ARDEN GREY

ARDEN GREY

Ray Stoeve

AMULET BOOKS
NEW YORK

Cataloging-in-Publication Data has been applied for and may be obtained from the Library of Congress.

ISBN 978-1-4197-4600-0

Text copyright © 2022 Ray Stoeve
Book design by Hana Anouk Nakamura

Printed and bound in U.S.A.
10 9 8 7 6 5 4 3 2 1

Amulet Books are available at special discounts when purchased in quantity for premiums and promotions as well as fundraising or educational use. Special editions can also be created to specification. For details, contact specialsales@abramsbooks.com or the address below.

Amulet Books® is a registered trademark of Harry N. Abrams, Inc.

ABRAMS The Art of Books
195 Broadway, New York, NY 10007
abramsbooks.com

*To queer friendships, in all their
magical and life-giving forms*

CHAPTER ONE

JAMIE IS TRYING TO CHEER ME UP AGAIN.

"Imagine Tanner gets caught in a wrestling hold the wrong way and his arm is slowly twisted off," he says. He grips the pull-up bar in his bedroom doorway, feet dangling in midair above the carpet. I grimace. Tanner may be the worst human in the world, but grievous bodily harm isn't my style.

"An expression! Ladies, gentlemen, and nonbinary honored guests, I see an actual facial expression." His wide smile answers my frown. Another pull-up.

I stare out the window at the October rain lashing the glass, the sky a single shade of pale gray. Seattle living up to its stereotype. Jamie grunts from the doorway, biceps flexing as he rises and lowers, face almost as red as his ginger hair. This is probably the kind of thing some people find hot, watching a guy work out. Not me. Jamie and I have been best friends since freshman year of high school, and sometimes people think we're dating, but that's just weird. I don't like anyone like that. Not boys or girls or anyone else. Why would I need to date when I have friends?

Okay, one friend. But the point stands. I'm not interested in any of that stuff—not romance, not sex.

In the doorway, Jamie blows air like an orca surfacing, his pull-ups slowing down.

"Are you done yet?" I ask.

"Nope. Gotta get those muscles. Make the most of that testosterone." Another pull-up. "Hashtag trans guy life."

"Hashtag trans formation," I say as his chin barely clears the bar.

"She's cracking jokes now, folks! My work here is done." He lowers himself to the floor and bounds across the room, flopping onto the bed next to me. "So what are we watching tonight?"

I let him scroll through Netflix until he finds some mindless action movie. This time it's *Point Break*, some classic from the eighties, maybe the nineties, I'm not sure. Jamie loves old movies.

The screen goes black, the production company logos fade in and out, and the first scene begins. We're going to be up way too late watching, but it doesn't matter. I'm always tired now, like my body is a suit of armor I can't take off.

Sometimes I wonder when I'm going to cry. I haven't yet. Not even the day it happened.

It was September, the third day of school. I'd just gotten home to find Mom and Dad in the kitchen, sitting on opposite sides of the counter but not talking to each other, their faces still and serious.

"What's wrong?" I asked. Mom always worked late, and Dad usually got home after me, so I knew something was up.

"Honey, could you go sit in the dining room please? We need to talk to you and Garrett about something," Dad said. His smile looked painted on.

I did what he asked. He called Garrett down and they took seats across from the two of us.

"Evelyn, do you want to . . ." Dad trailed off, looking at her.

Mom nodded. She looked at us, her eyes clear. "Your dad and I are separating for a while. Things haven't been working between us for a long time, and I'm going to go stay with a friend in San Francisco while we take some space."

She folded her hands, watching us, like it was the most normal thing in the world to say. Like she'd just told us we were going on vacation, not that our family was ending. I knew I was supposed to say something, but I couldn't think of anything. My whole body was frozen.

"You're getting a divorce?" Garrett said finally. His voice sounded like he was choking.

"No, just separating. We need some time to think about what's next," Mom said.

"Uh huh." He pushed back his chair so hard it fell against the wall. Dad flinched. Mom usually would have snapped at him, but she just watched. "Have fun in San Francisco." He spat the words at her and left, charging up the stairs to his room. A moment later, his door slammed.

I shut my eyes tight. That was a month ago, and I'm still thinking about it. What exactly stopped working for her? The marriage? The family? Did she leave because of her and Dad, or was it Garrett and me, too?

Jamie pokes me. "You okay?"

I look at him. His brown eyes are warm. I try a smile, manage a lips-closed line with the ends upturned. Good enough. "What did I miss?"

"Keanu's a new FBI agent and he's gonna help investigate this ring of bank robbers."

I nod and try to focus on the movie. I don't really care what's happening. The question is just an anchor, a way to hold myself in the moment. If I stay here, I won't think about back then.

Sometimes, when I wake up in the morning, I imagine that this will be the day I start over. I'm going to walk into school and be someone else, someone loud and funny, with a posse of friends. Someone who wears bright-colored clothes and dyes her hair and isn't afraid to speak up in class. Or speak up in general. But instead, I get up and put on jeans and a black t-shirt, comb my shoulder-length brownish-blond hair, and stare at my one eyeliner pencil before deciding, again, not to wear makeup. I don't know what I'm so afraid of. But not knowing doesn't make the fear go away.

On Monday before school, when I'm done with my daily emotional crisis, I sit on the steps and wait for Jamie's mom to pick me up. Most days I bus, but it's raining (surprise!) and Jamie texted to ask if I wanted a ride. I huddle under the awning on the front porch until they arrive. Jamie presses his face against the car window, smooshing his lips and cheek flat against the glass as I walk up to his old red minivan. Inside, heat blasts from the air vents and Heart wails from the speakers.

"Arden!" Jamie's mom Kim beams at me, then guns it away from the curb. She's cut her hair again, in what Jamie and I call the "Ellen DeGeneres": short, blond, and very, very gay. Jamie's other mom, Lisa, is more of a Ponytail Lesbian.

"Your hair looks nice," I say.

"You're so sweet. You always notice. Unlike some people," she says, arching an eyebrow at Jamie.

"You've been getting the same cut for three years," he says.

"Just wait. I'll come home with purple hair and then you'll really freak."

The day is a series of tests in Navigating the High School Hellscape: essay research in English, group work in French, an actual test in history, and biology. Yeah. Biology doesn't need to do anything special to suck. It exists in Permanent Trash World.

Mr. Bones (his actual real name, Jamie checked) passes out a worksheet on genotypes and phenotypes. I bend over my paper, leaning my head on one hand while I fill it out. Across the room, Tanner and his friends are joking and laughing. Some of the girls sit on their desks, legs crossed. When they talk, the boys watch them and look at each other like they know some secret the girls don't know. Tanner gestures wildly, words exploding from his mouth, interrupting Caroline Summers midsentence, and his buddies join in, all of them talking over each other. The girls laugh. Tanner looks over at me and catches my eye before I can look at my worksheet.

"Ar-den!" He singsongs my name like it's two words instead of one. I ignore him.

"Arden! Arden! Arden!" He's chanting my name now. The girls giggle. My heart beats like a washing machine and rage rises in my chest like dirty water, but I can't give in, can't give him the satisfaction.

"Tanner." Mr. Bones's voice echoes across the classroom and all chatter grinds to a halt. I stare at my worksheet but I'm not seeing it. "Office."

"I wasn't even doing anything, Mr. B!"

"Now, Mr. Olson."

I hear a heavy sigh and the exaggerated thumping of books into a backpack, and then the door opens and slams shut. I stare at my worksheet and focus on the rage, imagine it's a typhoon sucking Tanner down into the ocean and drowning him, his square white face swollen, stupid faux-hawk waving like seaweed. Maybe grievous bodily harm is my style after all. I focus on the rage and I don't cry. I don't cry. I don't cry. Around the room conversations bloom again, seeding through the desks until the noise level is back to normal. I avoid looking at anyone for the rest of the class.

The bell rings and right on cue, it's Mr. B with an *Arden could you stay a moment please?* Everyone else piles out the door like the floor is made of lava as I walk over to Mr. B's desk.

"How are you, Arden?" he asks when the classroom is empty.

I shrug. "I'm fine." I look at his desk, all the items organized into containers: paper clips in a small glass box, pens in a mason jar, papers filed neatly into an upright metal organizer divided by class period.

"What's the deal with you and Tanner?"

"Nothing."

"That didn't look like nothing."

I look up and meet his eyes, focused on me under the bushy eyebrows Jamie and I giggled about when we were freshmen. His gaze is laser-sharp, a microscope under which I am frozen. "How long has this been going on?" he asks.

"Last year," I mumble. I'm not about to tell him how it all started. Please god, don't let him ask. "It's really not a big deal. I just ignore him."

"Well, maybe other teachers have let it slide, but I want you to know it's not going to fly in my class." He steeples his fingers, gaze steady on me. "Please let me know if there's anything I can do."

I nod. I just want to get out of here.

He looks up at the clock. "Don't let me keep you from your lunch."

When I get home from school that afternoon, I'm tired. I'm achy all over and my head hurts like I'm getting sick. Maybe I am. I could take a shower and sit outside in the rain for a little bit, and then maybe I'll get sicker and I can stay home tomorrow.

I don't do that, though. I go into my room and lie down on the rug, earbuds in, and turn the music up as far as I can before it hurts my ears. I unfocus my eyes, watching the floaters slide down my retina, blinking them back up again and again, as Tegan and Sara sing in their jangly voices about a ghost.

As long as I can remember, I've done this. This lying-on-the-floor thing. Garrett, in all his thirteen-year-old little-brother wisdom, thinks it's weird. Why don't you just lie on the bed, he always asks. But there's something comforting about the floor, the shiny red-brown hardwood under the flat striped rug holding me up. The bed is too soft. Sometimes I like to lie underneath it, though. It feels safe there, closed-in, like nothing can get to me.

I fix my eyes on the white ceiling, shaded blue by the light blue walls, and drift away into my mind. Mom is waiting for me there. The morning of the day they told us, I saw her standing in her and Dad's bedroom, staring out the window. I stopped in the hallway and watched her, but she was somewhere else. I could have said good morning, but I didn't. It was easier to avoid her.

Sometimes when I think about her, I feel like she doesn't exist anymore. Not like she died; I'm sad, but I'm not morbid. No, it's just like she wasn't real, like maybe I imagined her. I know she was there, of course. She's in our pictures: holding me at a family reunion. Watching me take my first steps. Making a goofy face behind the candles on her birthday cake. For some of our pictures she was behind the camera, before she got too wrapped up in running a gallery for other people's photos instead of taking her own. But in my memories, she's a cardboard cutout, a mother-shaped space. Who was she, really? Who were we to each other? I don't know. The things I have, the things I remember, I hold tight in my fists like they'll vanish if I let go, the same way she did.

CHAPTER TWO

ON SATURDAY, THE LIGHT IS PERFECT, ALL HEAVY GRAY CLOUDS and no rain. It's a photo-adventure kind of day. Jamie and I take the train to downtown Seattle and get off in Pioneer Square. I have my Pentax K1000 with a fresh roll of black-and-white film inside it, and we wander through the alleys, admiring the old buildings and the trash and the graffiti. Jamie leans against a brick wall, fixing his eyes on a point in the distance.

"Oh, glamour! Yes, darling," I say, snapping a picture. "That's the shot." His face twitches, trying to hold still and serious, but his mouth has other ideas and a grin breaks loose across his face. The click of the shutter gets it. Hand through his hair. Click. Eyes crossed, cheeks puffed out. Click. Close-up of the ivy curling down the brick. Click.

I've been taking pictures since Mom and Dad gave me the Pentax for my twelfth birthday. I thought it was stupid at first—why use film when my phone can take five hundred perfect digital pictures with one ten-second press of the touch screen? So the camera sat on my desk in my room for months, gathering a fine coat of dust.

Then one Saturday morning I came to breakfast and found the camera sitting on my plate. Mom was away consulting for a gallery opening in San Francisco and Dad seemed more relaxed than usual, humming along with the radio while he scrambled eggs in a skillet. I picked the camera up. It was dust-free.

"I thought we could go out shooting today," he said. He'd always liked to take pictures, but for him, it was a hobby. For Mom, it was art.

"Are those blueberry?" I asked as he tipped a steaming stack of pancakes onto my plate.

"You got it. I'm not above bribery."

We spent most of the day downtown at Pike Place Market, exploring all the tiny shops winding down like a warren into the hillside overlooking the Puget Sound. Dad showed me Post Alley and the wall covered in gum, pretending to lick it as I squealed in disgust and snapped a photo. We used up the whole roll and dropped it off for development on the way home.

When the pictures came back a week later, I stared at the photo of Dad until I could see every detail in my mind. He looked happy, curly brown hair a wild nest in the October wind, tongue almost touching a piece of chewed gum mashed to the wall. The rubber-duck yellow of the gum matched his raincoat. I could smell the fish from the seafood booths nearby, hear the chatter of tourists, the day unfolding in my memory like a movie. The colors of the photo were brighter than digital, unmanipulated by a filter, the slight grain of the film adding a richness and depth none of my Instagram posts had ever captured. I didn't have a photo of every moment from that day, but I didn't need them. This photo was the day, in one single moment.

I started using the camera more. And by more, I mean it went everywhere with me: tucked into my backpack at school, slung across my shoulder on trips to the grocery store, hanging around my neck as I wandered around our neighborhood waiting for something to catch my eye.

After a while, taking photos with my phone was the thing that seemed stupid. The Pentax wouldn't let me take a million photos of the same thing and delete every imperfect image before posting it to my Instagram where I'd never look at it again—and I liked that. With film, every image meant something. There were no do-overs.

Every photo was permanent, a moment frozen forever, unchangeable, undeletable, honest. Hashtag no filter. No one can say it didn't happen if you have a photograph of it. But I don't show my photos to anyone, except Dad and Jamie. It feels safer somehow. I don't know from what, but that part is important.

Jamie and I wander through Pioneer Square to Occidental Park, a plaza sprawled out in front of an old building, both made of red brick, the building's face covered in a layer of green ivy. A few men in big coats and ragged shoes huddle at one end. We cross the plaza and Jamie leaps up on a lamppost straight out of *Singin' in the Rain*, flinging out his arm for the photo.

We walk up through downtown and then turn right on Pike Street, starting the trek back up to my house in Capitol Hill. I love taking pictures in the city, love the whirl of faces and colors and textures, how the movement of people pulls me out of my head and into a place where I notice details no one else does. When I'm taking pictures, I am nowhere else but here, in the moment, in the image. Nothing else matters.

By the time we're back at my house, the black-and-white roll is finished and the rain is starting. I load in a color roll while Jamie uses the bathroom at the end of the hall.

"Shit!" he says, voice ringing through the closed door. I walk out of my room, laughing. "I mean, not actual shit, I'm just peeing in here. I forgot to do my shot this morning. Can we go to my house?"

I answer an affirmative, pressing the back of the camera closed and winding the film forward.

We leave, running for the bus stop in the downpour. It's one of those sudden, heavy fall rains, here and then over in minutes. My house is on the west side of the Hill, close enough to walk to Broadway, the main street through the neighborhood. Jamie's house is further east, down in the valley near Lake Washington. When we arrive, the rain has stopped—clouds rolling across the sky, sun peeking through and brightening the sidewalk for seconds at a time.

In his bedroom, Jamie assembles his supplies for his testosterone shot. I've seen him do it a hundred times, but I've never thought to take a picture.

"Can I?" I ask, holding up the camera.

"Sure." He's focused on the T in its tiny bottle, upended on the needle as he draws it out. I stand on the carpet in front of him and lift the camera. Click. He removes the vial, switches the needle out for a smaller one, and buries it in the fat on his stomach.

"My manniversary is coming up," he says as he pushes the testosterone, suspended in golden oil, out of the needle and under his skin.

"I can't believe you've been on T for a year," I say, sitting cross-legged on the floor in front of him. "We should celebrate."

He pulls the needle out, tossing it into the sharps container under his nightstand, the rest of the waste going into the garbage can beside it. He grins at me. "Hell yeah."

We waste a few hours watching cartoons. Lisa and Kim get home and rustle around in the house, their voices a comforting white noise. Jamie's little sister is at ballet lessons, already a prodigy at nine years old. Their house feels like my house, if my house had been a place where the parents cooked together and laughed and watched television shows as a family.

Even though we did. We did all the same things other families did, but somehow it felt like we were different. Like we were all holding a secret, one we couldn't even talk about with each other. Like every happy moment was a glass on the edge of breaking.

Lisa pokes her head in, long brown ponytail swinging over her shoulder. "Arden, you staying for dinner?" Her voice is always raspy, like she's pushing it out from somewhere deep in her stomach.

"Sure." I smile and she smiles back, eyes lingering a little too long on mine. She's looked at me that way ever since the day Mom and Dad told us and I showed up on their doorstep unannounced, unable to speak, only able to write out what had happened.

I look away at the characters yelling and fighting on the computer screen. After a moment, Lisa leaves.

::

People talk about depression as if it's the same thing as negativity. As if I'm a character in a Sunday newspaper comic, walking around with a little dark cloud over my head, bringing everyone down with my pessimism.

Depression isn't a dark cloud. It's an anchor, an ocean, a weight. The thing I'm drowning in and the thing holding me under at the same time. It's a sadness so deep that I've stopped feeling sad and just feel the absence of sadness instead. The only time I feel anything is when I'm with Jamie, or when I'm out with my camera.

It wasn't always this way. I don't think this depression is only about my brain chemistry, the way we learned about it in health class. I know I've been happy before. But since Mom left, I've had trouble remembering if I ever was.

I think Dad is the same. I don't know for sure, because he doesn't talk to us about Mom, but since she left, he's retreated. When he smiles at me and Garrett, he smiles from somewhere far back behind his eyes, like he's a distant star and we're planets light-years away.

Garrett hasn't retreated. Garrett isn't drowning.

Sunday evening finds me studying at the dining room table, him in front of the living room television, lost in his new favorite first-person shooter.

"Goddamn it!" He throws his controller on the floor.

I jump and stare at him over my laptop. He mumbles more curses as he stomps past me to the kitchen and rattles around in the cabinets for a snack. When he glances over and sees me, still staring at him from the dining room table, he raises his eyebrows.

"What?"

"It's a video game, Garrett."

"It's a video game, Garrett!" He pitches his voice higher than usual.

I roll my eyes and look back at my screen. There's no point in arguing with him, and I don't have the energy to try. He's extra loud in the kitchen now, yanking doors open and slamming them shut, plunking a bowl down on the counter and shaking chips into it, but I ignore him. I know he's just trying to get to me.

Garrett wasn't always an asshole. It's a new thing, like something he's trying on, a style he picked up from his middle-school buddies. I'm not a fan, and neither was Mom. When he'd curse at his game or get mad at her for not letting him do something, she'd just look at him and turn away. No matter what he did after that, she'd ignore him until he apologized.

She never ignored me. But I tried to never give her a reason to. Arguing with her was never worth it. Arguing always made things worse.

"She was so pretty before," Mom had said once last year, one of the few times I'd brought Jamie over to the house. Her words sliced through me, a knife in my back as I walked to my bedroom after closing the front door behind him.

I turned to face her. She sat on the couch, a blueprint for a new exhibition at the gallery laid out on the coffee table.

"He," I said. "He doesn't care about being pretty."

"I just don't understand how Kim and Lisa can put their child on medication like that," she said, as if I hadn't spoken. "What if it's just a phase?"

"That's not how it works, Mom," I said, tucking my hands into the pockets of my hoodie.

"There's no need to be rude," she said, looking up at me.

"I'm not trying to be rude," I said carefully. Quietly. "Jamie's so much happier now. His moms know what they're doing."

"And I don't?"

I frowned. "That's not what I'm saying."

"You think I should just say yes to whatever you want?" She shook her head. "You're a teenager, Arden. You wouldn't even be able to feed yourself if it wasn't for me. There's no way you're equipped to make the kind of decision Jamie's making."

Dad feeds us, too, I wanted to say. He's the one who cooks. His money buys our groceries just as much as yours. Jamie's transition isn't a decision, or at least not a casual one.

"I'm sorry," I said instead.

"Sorry for what?" Her eyes were back on her blueprint.

"For being rude."

"I accept your apology," she said.

The laptop screen refocuses in front of me. I've been staring at the same paragraph on the same webpage for five minutes now. Garrett is back in front of the television, numb to the world. I take a deep breath, then another, the dark water of memory swirling around me. Arguments with Mom always left me feeling that way, like I was floundering, searching for land I could have sworn was there a second ago, not sure how I ended up so far out in the current.

Three days after that moment in the living room, Mom refused to sign the permission form for a class field trip. We were going to the art museum for a photography exhibit. She knew I was looking forward to it. And I knew, when she said no, that this was the rest of my punishment. Even though, when I really thought about it, I knew I hadn't been rude.

But what I thought didn't matter. The only thing that mattered was how she saw it.

The week brings November, and with it CandyGram season on a wave of whispers and giggles. The freshmen girls line up to buy Grams by the stack, sending one to all their friends plus their crush, if they're brave enough. The paper cutouts litter the hallways: ground underfoot, pasted to lockers, piled in the trash. It's the same design every year: candy canes in a heart shape, framing a prewritten message with a piece of candy taped below. On Thursday, I buy Jamie one, because we always do that, and slip away from the table just in time to avoid being seen by Tanner. No way do I want to give him any ammo. I can hear it now: "Whoa whoa whoa, Arden has a crush?! I thought you were asexual. Guess now you're a SEXUAL!" Cue hysterical laughter.

Tanner never paid much attention to me freshman year. I thought he was annoying and stupid, but I thought that about most of the guys he was friends with, too. They played the sports no one cared about but with the egos of football players, and they thought their jokes and pranks were the second coming of comedy. Second coming, ha ha ha, they might say, moaning in case no one got it. Even though everyone got it.

But he ignored me and I ignored him. Until the end of last year. We were learning about sexual orientation in sophomore health class and our teacher (Mr. Feldman, second-most Politically Aware Teacher in the school, after the history teacher, Ms. Maldonado) was talking about the LGBT acronym. Specifically, the rest of it: QIAP, etcetera, etcetera.

Vanessa Flores, the secretary of the Queer Alliance, was expounding on the meaning of asexuality, and I found myself nodding. I could relate to it. And I'd always wanted to go to the QA meetings but was too intimidated. Everyone in QA seemed impossibly cool, especially Vanessa and her lipsticks, a different color for every day of the week.

The next week when people were buying tickets for the spring dance, Tanner and his buddies were hassling every girl who came into class, asking them about their date status. When he shouted at me from across the room, I ignored him. He repeated the question. And then: "What are you, Arden, asexual? Have you ever even been to a dance?"

I dropped into my seat, but the blush turned my face hot and I knew he saw it, because he started cackling, shoving back and forth with his buddies the way guys do when they think they've said something clever.

It was all over after that. Or rather, that was just the beginning.

I lose myself behind a crowd of shrieking freshmen and head down senior hall. You can either deliver the Gram yourself or have it delivered to the recipient's class by cheerleaders dressed as elves, and the recipient can then pay a dollar to find out who sent it. All the money funds the winter dance. I don't care about that, so I find Jamie at his locker and hand it to him without ceremony. He rips the wrapper off the attached peppermint patty, shoving the whole thing into his mouth. From him, I get one with a peanut butter cup, my favorite.

In math class, everybody's talking loudly, hopped up on sugar and the excitement of secret crushes. I don't really understand why it's so exciting, and apparently our math teacher doesn't either, because she spends ten minutes yelling at us about our test scores and almost drops an F-bomb when she catches a girl from the soccer team passing a Gram to her friend. She snatches it and tosses it in the trash.

The door bursts open and two cheerleaders in Santa hats strike a pose. "CandyGram delivery!" The teacher rolls her eyes but motions them in, and they prance through the aisles. A few people get one: The soccer girl squeals as they drop one on her desk, and a football player in the corner blushes bright red as they hand him three. Then they turn to Jamie and hand him a Gram.

Jamie? I stare at him and he stares down at the Gram. The football player turns around.

"Way to go, man," he says, lifting one massive hand for a high five. He looks disappointed at Jamie's lackluster return five, barely a graze of the palm, Jamie's eyes still fixed on the Gram.

The cheerleaders leave and the teacher drags us reluctantly into the math lesson. Jamie swivels his head slowly, arching an eyebrow at me. I shake my head. *Who is it*, he mouths. I shrug. He peels the mini chocolate bar off the paper, eating it slowly as he stares up at the board.

I wonder who sent it to him. Jamie's only dated once, in middle school, before we met, but I know he wants a girlfriend. He has a crush on a new girl practically every month. Miss November is Mina Ishimura, a senior and the cheer captain. He always goes for the unattainable ones.

When the last bell rings we leave class, heading for our lockers.

"Who do you think it was?" I ask.

"No idea," he says. "But I'm definitely dropping a dollar to find out."

"Maybe it's someone's idea of a joke," I say, and then regret the words instantly as he frowns at me.

"Right, because no one could have a crush on me?" he asks.

"That's not what I meant." I grip the straps of my backpack tighter. "I'm sorry. That came out wrong. I just mean,

I don't know. I hope it's real." My voice disappears and he squeezes my elbow.

"It's okay."

Is it? I walk beside him in silence the rest of the way to our lockers, as he high-fives other dudes from the basketball team, says hello to a few teachers standing outside their classrooms, and grabs a piece of unwanted candy tossed to him from a girl I don't recognize. The silent, shy Jamie who took the last empty seat beside me in freshman-year English is gone, and I'm glad. But sometimes I wonder how much longer this Jamie will stick around with me, still shy, still silent.

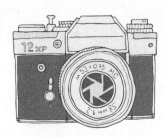

CHAPTER THREE

"CAROLINE SUMMERS." JAMIE SITS DOWN IN FRONT OF ME IN second period the next day.

"What about her?"

"The CandyGram. She's in my English class. We were in the same group for the *King Lear* project." He opens Instagram on his phone and shows me a picture. She's smiling, standing in front of the Grand Canyon. She's white, like me and Jamie, but in the picture she's tanned, hair in one long brunette braid over her shoulder.

"She looks like she could be in an outdoor gear ad," I say.

"I know, right? She's cute as fuck," Jamie says, smiling down at his phone.

"What are you going to do?"

He shrugged. "Talk to her, I guess. Say hi. She seemed

cool when we were doing the project. She always says something smart in class."

"Do you like her?"

One corner of his mouth lifts. "Mina's still my number one. But Caroline . . ." He wiggles his eyebrows. "Who knows? Anything could happen."

I take notes as the teacher writes an equation on the board, but I'm not listening. I've barely talked to Caroline, even though we've had classes together. Like bio, this year. She's always surrounded by soccer team girls, laughing about something. I wonder when she started liking Jamie, what it was that made her send the Gram. I know Jamie's great, of course, but when I realized that in freshman year, I had just made friends with him. I've never had a crush. At least, not on someone I could actually date. There are celebrities I think are cute. Ones I've loved so much I've imagined us on dates or holding hands. Which maybe means I do care about romance. But the idea of dating someone in my real life makes my brain itch and my stomach turn over. If I dated someone, they might want to kiss, which wouldn't be terrible. (I think.) But then they'd probably want to do other things. Most people seem to want to. But I never have, and I can't picture that changing.

In bed that night, I tap through my Google Calendar, checking out what homework is due next week. A box pops up for Friday night: JAMIE'S ONE YEAR ON T. Right. We talked about that.

I text him. your manniversary is Friday. what do you wanna do?

ONE WEEK BABY! Um idk. movie night?

we ALWAYS do movie night. you've been on t a whole year!

we could burn my bras?

you STILL have them???? wow jamie

lol says the girl who has every photo she's ever taken since age 12

PLEASE. those are HISTORICAL ARTIFACTS. when i'm as famous as Annie Leibovitz, people will be fighting over that shit

mhmmmmm well last I checked Annie Leibovitz actually shows her photos to people

I send a GIF: Boromir in the last scene of *The Fellowship of the Ring*, getting hit by arrow after arrow. But it does sting. I have my reasons for not showing anyone my photos. Whenever I've let someone besides Dad and Jamie see them, it hasn't gone well.

The first photo I ever took that I was proud of was from my first roll of black-and-white film. Garrett was ten, and I'd just turned thirteen. In the photo, he's swinging from a limb on the apple tree behind our house. The blossoms are in full bloom, a cloud of pure white, and he's mid-swing, his legs a blur, his face in focus, gap-toothed smile blazing into the lens.

"The composition is off," Mom said when I showed it to her. "He should be centered."

Dad had been there when she'd said it, and he'd leaned in to look. "I think that looks great, actually."

Mom was silent. I looked up at him and he smiled. "It might not be perfect, but it doesn't have to be," he said. "The emotion really comes through."

After that, I kept trying to show Mom my photos, but she had a critique for every single one. It was like, the moment they gave me the camera, she'd decided in her mind that I was the family artist, and she'd mold me into one by force of her words alone. Every so often, there'd be something she'd like about one of my pictures, but after a while I stopped showing her and went to Dad instead. And she never asked to see what I was working on; she was always busy. Her whole life was the gallery. She'd opened it the same year I got the camera, after she left her position as executive director at the Seattle Art Museum. I still remember opening night. I had to wear a dress, and Dad and Garrett wore suits, and we smiled and stayed quiet like a model family while she schmoozed with all these rich-looking adults. I knew we were better off than a lot of my classmates, but these people were a whole different level.

It wasn't so bad, that first year. She seemed happy. But eventually, she started spending more and more time there, and then she started consulting on the side, traveling to other museums and galleries to advise on curation and speak on panels. When she was home, she and Dad hardly spoke. At the time, I was relieved. They'd fought all the time when I was younger, sometimes yelling, sometimes in cold silence that was somehow worse than the yelling. I thought they were finally okay, that we would start being happy like Jamie's family.

But now I wonder: Was that the beginning of the end?

A text pings my phone. I shake my head, as if I can shake off the memory, and open it.

so we on for Friday?

definitely, I text back.

Sunday is nothing but studying for the French test. Jamie comes over and Dad goes grocery shopping, leaving us in the living room, notes spread out on the coffee table.

Jamie's leg is shaking up and down, and he keeps spacing out, or grabbing his phone just to look at the screen and put it down again. After about the tenth time in two minutes, I put down my flashcards.

"Dude. What is going on?"

He looks at me, a grin sneaking onto his face. "I got her number."

"Who?"

"Caroline!"

"Oh, right." He's still smiling at me. I'm supposed to say something. "So, uh, did you text her?"

He holds up his phone. "Hell yeah, I did. We've been texting all weekend."

His grin is contagious, and I can't help smiling. He looks so excited. Caroline must be great if she makes him light up this way.

"She's so cool, Arden. She plays basketball and soccer, too, and she's super funny. She's seen every show on Adult Swim. We quoted *Rick and Morty* back and forth for literally an hour. Complete with GIFs." His cheeks are pink, eyes bright.

Jamie knows I hate Adult Swim. All of those shows seem so crude. But now he can share it with Caroline. Something clangs inside my chest, but I quiet it instantly. Jamie's my best friend. I have nothing to worry about.

"You should ask her out," I say.

"On it." He points a finger-gun at me. "Asked this morning if she wanted to go for coffee after school Friday. I'm just waiting to hear back."

Friday. "What about your manniversary?"

"Shit." He looks at his phone, then back at me, his face scrunching up. "I'll change the day."

"No!" The word pops out of my mouth before I can stop it. "No. That's okay. We can do it Saturday night."

"Are you sure?" His face unscrunches. I nod, grinning as big as I can. "Awesome. Awesome. You're the best." He looks at his phone again and jumps a little, swiping open the text on the lock screen.

Dad comes back a little while later, kicking the door to let us know his hands are full. We help him carry the grocery bags in from the station wagon and put the food away.

"Got these on my way home." He slips a thick envelope into my hand: the photos from the Pioneer Square adventure.

"Thanks, Dad." I hug him, and he hugs back, the thick wool of his sweater scratchy against my cheek.

"I'll be in my room if you two need anything," he says and releases me. I watch him disappear out of the kitchen and my heart aches suddenly, like someone is squeezing it. He spends a lot of time in his room now. Sometimes I hear music playing, but mostly it's quiet, and I've never interrupted him to find out what he's doing. Part of me doesn't want to know. I want my smiling dad from the Post Alley gum wall, not this quiet dad who hugs me like he's trying to say something without words.

"Arden! I need you! *S'il vous plaît!*" Jamie howls from the living room. I appear in the doorway to see him lying upside down on the couch, head dangling toward the floor. "Do you think if I stay in this position long enough all the vocabulary words will pool in my brain and stay there?"

"That's stupid." I roll my eyes.

He clutches his chest in mock outrage, then swings his legs down and stands up. "Oh. Head rush." He sits back down heavily.

"That's just your brain processing knowledge," I say, sitting down at the coffee table.

"No, I think that's my brain telling me it's time to eat." He runs to the kitchen and returns with a bag of chips. I take the photos out of the envelope and spread them over our notes.

"That's the headshot for my future modeling career," Jamie says, pointing over my shoulder at the shot of him in the alley, cheeks puffed out and eyes crossed. I snort and keep sifting through them. Most of them are good, but nothing with a special spark; just shots of a fun day out. He picks up a black-and-white of the Smith Tower jutting into heavy clouds. "Nice angle. You should submit this somewhere. There's gotta be magazines for this stuff."

I shrug. "None of these are good enough."

"Shut up." He pushes my shoulder with his knee. "That's not true. You've got the eye."

Now I'm looking at the color roll. I finished it last week, and it's mostly shots from school: the hallways swirling with students, the flag rippling over the building, a football player sitting in a stairwell in full uniform.

"Whoa," Jamie says, and then I see it, too: the photo of him doing his shot. The angle is perfect, his eyes fastened to the needle, the background blurred around him. The colors are warm but not too saturated.

A few feet away on the coffee table, his phone lights up with another text, but he doesn't pick it up.

The clock ticks over the kitchen doorway. I look at the picture and remember the quiet safety of Jamie's room.

"That's the one," he says, and I nod. There's a keeper in every roll, and this is it.

CHAPTER FOUR

WE'RE STANDING AT JAMIE'S LOCKER MONDAY MORNING WHEN his eyes shift over my shoulder. I turn and look. It's Caroline, a group of friends around her.

"Hey," Jamie says as she passes, smiling, jerking his chin up in a nod. It's a move I've seen straight guys do before. To each other, no smile, just a hallway acknowledgment. Or with a smile halfway between a smirk and a grin, to girls they like. But this is the first time I've seen Jamie do it.

"Hi, Jamie," Caroline says over her shoulder, giving a little wave. Her friends close around her, all giggles and shoulder pushes and hands over mouths as they walk away. Jamie shoves his hands in his pockets, beaming after them. They keep looking back, laughter pealing out anew every time. Caroline swats at one of them but doesn't look back.

"Yup. She definitely likes me." Jamie turns to his locker, smiling into the pile of books.

I look back again. She's gone in the swirling, faceless maelstrom. Watching her, watching him, is like reading another language. I can see when people like each other. It's in their body language. But I don't know how to make my body communicate that way. And I've never met anyone I wanted to speak with.

Jamie floats from moment to moment that week, texting me when Caroline smiles at him in class, or when she reveals yet another thing they have in common (her lesbian aunt and his lesbian moms; younger sisters; a fixation on the same Seattle Sounders soccer player).

are you sure you're not actually the same person, I ask him over text Wednesday night.

i mean, i'm pretty great. i'd date myself, he says back. Usually his bravado makes me laugh, because I know what's underneath it. I know how hard it was for him to get to a place where he could say that. But tonight it just annoys me. I wish I had his confidence.

I toss the phone across my room onto my bed and spin in my desk chair. It's late, almost ten, around the time Dad usually knocks on my door and tells me to go to bed, but he hasn't shown up yet. I stare at the poster above my desk:

a portrait by Annie Leibovitz, from her "Women" exhibition, given to me by Mom for Christmas one year. In it, the softball player is mid-throw, arm cocked back, body pulled open like a bow, right leg sweeping a clean line forward from her chin to the ground. The kind of photo Mom loved. "A symbol of female power and endurance," she ruminated once.

I don't know about that. I don't know if I even believe in female or male anymore. Biological sex is kind of meaningless when you think about it. Why do body parts somehow symbolize gender? Makes no sense. Jamie's a guy. I'm a girl. Body parts have nothing to do with it. It's how we feel inside.

If it were me picking a woman I want to be like, I wouldn't choose a softball player. Below the poster are smaller pictures, portraits, ones I wish I'd taken, ripped from magazines. In the center, Hayley Kiyoko's shoot for *Nylon*. She stands with rolls of colored paper behind her, hands clasped in front of her, huge jacket falling open to reveal one half of her bra. But it's her eyes that get me. She's not just looking at the camera. She's looking through it, as if she's checking out every girl who sees her, flirting with just her gaze.

"Why do you have gay porn on your wall?" Garrett asked when I put the photo up in June.

"Just because she's a lesbian in a bra doesn't mean it's porn." I rolled my eyes at him. Of all the things I don't want to discuss with my thirteen-year-old brother, porn and my sexuality are at the top of the list.

He just snorted, muttered an *okayyyy*, and slid away from my door and down the hall.

But Hayley Kiyoko is gorgeous. I'll give him that. I might even say she's hot, except "hot" feels like a word someone would use if they wanted to do it with the person they were talking about. And I don't want to have sex with her. I just want to cuddle and talk and maybe kiss.

This is what's confusing to me. I get crushes. I have romantic feelings for people. For girls—it's always girls. Laverne Cox smiles at me from beside Hayley, and next to her, Janelle Monae. Liking girls isn't really a big deal to me. At least, not when they're celebrities. But a girl I could actually date? One who would want to cuddle and talk and kiss, and maybe other things, too, things I know I don't want, the same way I know what I do want?

Terrifying.

My stomach growls and I push away from the desk,

heading out to the kitchen for a snack. Chips and hummus. I'm carrying the food back to my room, past Dad's bedroom, when I hear his voice. The door is open a crack, and I pause.

"I don't understand, Evelyn." His voice is gravelly. Evelyn. He's talking to Mom.

Then silence. I want more than anything to peek around the door, look at him, but I don't. He never told us he was talking to Mom again. Or still. Maybe they never stopped talking. Maybe they've been talking this whole time.

"What about the kids?" he says.

I can't hear her end of the conversation, and I don't want to know what he says next. A hundred possibilities bubble up in my brain, none of them nice, my heart clenching tight like a fist. I back away, shutting my door quietly. How can she talk to him but not to us? Tears blur my vision, but I blink them back, grabbing my laptop and burrowing into my bed.

The day they told us, after Garrett's door slammed, I unfroze enough to get up, put on my shoes, and walk out of the house, even though I'd just gotten home from school. I walked all the way to Jamie's house, sweating under the early September sun. Lisa opened the door, smiled at me,

42

called into the house for Jamie. When she turned back and I was still standing there, silent, staring straight ahead, she reached out. Touched my shoulder. Asked if I was okay. I shook my head. But I didn't cry. She led me to their dining room table, sat me down. Jamie appeared, asked me questions, but all I could do was shake my head when every guess was wrong. Finally, Lisa set paper and pen in front of me, sat down beside him. Out of the corner of my eye, I saw them look at each other as I wrote it down: *Mom is leaving us.*

When I finally went home that night, dinner was over, and Dad and Garrett were sitting in the living room, Garrett red-eyed. Dad heated up a piece of the lasagna Mom had made for us the night before and brought it out for me, while Garrett sat there silently. Dad reached out and squeezed my hand, but I didn't answer the question in his eyes.

Mom left a few days later, and then we didn't talk about it again.

The next morning, it's like Dad's voice got stuck on autoloop in my head. *I don't understand, what about the kids, I don't understand, what about the kids what about the kids what about the kids*—I slam my locker door and lean my forehead against the cold metal. Shut up, brain.

"You okay?"

I look up and see Jamie, frown creasing his forehead. "Yeah. Just tired."

"Arden." He looks at me for a long moment.

"I'm fine." The last word comes out louder than I intended. Jamie raises an eyebrow, but he doesn't press me for once. The bell rings and we head to class.

"So how's your giiiiirlfriend?" I ask, more to distract him than because I'm actually interested.

He laughs. "She's not my girlfriend. Yet."

"Someone's feeling confident."

"Well, she asked me to sit with her at lunch today, so yeah, I'm feeling pretty good." He doesn't look at me as he says this, sliding ahead into the classroom. And I feel like a terrible person for this, but the first thing I think is: What about me?

"That's cool," I say instead.

"You should come, too," he says.

"Are you sure?"

"Duh. I need you there. You're my wingwoman." He grins, and I feel a little better.

By lunchtime, my stomach feels like it's caving in, and not because I'm hungry. Jamie and I never eat in the lunchroom. We're usually out in a hallway somewhere or sitting out front watching the skateboarders grind down the railings in front of the school. I haven't set foot in the cafeteria since the first week of freshman year.

But here we are. The double doors are propped wide open, voices swirling out into the hall like a current that grabs us and sucks us in. The cafeteria is vast, tables everywhere, with the kitchen at one end with a line of students snaking out of it. I follow Jamie, trying not to look as nauseous as I feel. Who is Caroline even friends with? I don't know any of the girls who circle her like they're her own personal planets.

Jamie stops and I almost bump into him. He smiles down at a table full of girls.

"We saved you a seat!" one of them shrieks, pointing at the one right next to Caroline.

Caroline smiles up at him, lips pressed together like she's hiding something behind them, something she only wants to give Jamie.

"This is Arden," Jamie says, and I step up beside him. Lift a hand. Smile. Try not to be a complete robot. "She's my best friend."

Caroline's smile wilts for a second. Maybe. It happens so fast, I think I might have made it up. Maybe I just want her to be mean to me. Then I'd have a reason to dislike her.

I don't dislike her. It's too soon for that.

"That's so cute," another girl says. She's blond, exactly like the first one who spoke, with shiny braces. "Guys and girls should be friends more often." She reaches back to the table right behind them and pulls a chair over. "You can sit here, Arden."

The chair is across the table from Jamie. Caroline's smile is back at full wattage. If it was ever really dimmed.

"Sure," I say, and go to the chair. I look at Jamie as he sits, and he grins at me, lifting his eyebrows just barely, as if to say, Look at us sitting here! Isn't this great?

I lift mine back, and I know what he'll think I'm saying. But inside I'm thinking, Great for who?

Lunch is a blur. I smile and nod in the right places as Blond Braces chatters away to me. She doesn't seem to need much encouragement. The other girls mostly ignore me, talking to each other, or to Caroline and Jamie. The two of them keep laughing, recounting the latest episode of some show they both like. From where I'm sitting, the show sounds stupid. And if I'm being honest, a little sexist and racist. Usually Jamie is really good about noticing any kind of -ism in a show or a movie. But he just laughs along with her.

The bell rings and I gather my stuff, mumbling good-bye to Braces. Around me, the other girls are rising from their seats. Jamie and I have different classes, and he's still talking to Caroline.

"See you later, everyone," I say, pitching my voice over the din. A few of the girls look at me. Jamie glances up and waves with a smile before looking back at Caroline.

If I stand here too long, it'll get awkward. I turn and lose myself in the river of students flowing out the doors, letting shoulders and bodies buffet me into the hall. It's fine. I don't have to go everywhere with Jamie. He's his own person, and so am I.

It's fine.

The next day dawns dark and stormy, exactly how I feel inside, because I'm a walking cliché, apparently. The rain pours nonstop the whole school day, clouds so thick and gray they're almost green. It's the day of Jamie's date with Caroline.

"I thought maybe we could sit with her at lunch again," he says during morning break.

I don't want to, and I take the huge mouthful of granola bar I'm chewing on as an excuse not to answer for a minute. "I'm going to go to the library," I say. "Gonna study."

"Aw shit, did I forget about a test again?"

"No, no." I shake my head. "I just want to get a jump on research for that English essay." That's a lie. I'm almost done with my research.

"Gotcha. No worries!" Jamie says with a smile. "I'll tell you all about it later. After my daaaate." He sings the word, wiggling his shoulders.

We should be prepping for his anniversary tonight instead. Even though we couldn't have a bonfire anyway with this rain. But whatever. I smile and try to look interested in what he's saying about Caroline until the bell rings and I escape to third period.

After school, I power walk to the bus stop, staring out the window all the way home. Jamie didn't meet me at my locker like usual because he was at Caroline's, which of course he would be. It doesn't matter. I have two good hours of light left and I'm going out to take some pictures.

The house is quiet when I get home. Garrett is at soccer practice for his select team; Dad is still at work.

He's a teacher, but not at our schools. Not that I would mind. But he told us a long time ago that our school years would be a "formative experience" and he didn't want to interfere with that for us. Which is exactly the kind of thing Dad would say. So he teaches English and history at a high school in South Seattle, and we go to school in North Seattle—Garrett at the same middle school I went to, me at Jefferson High. Home of the Salmon, which I wouldn't even know if not for Jamie. *Splish splash, get that cash, we fight, we score, we win it fast.* Alternate, non-school-approved ending: *we kick your ass.* Either way, it isn't even a full rhyme.

I exhale a groan into the empty kitchen, grabbing a snack. I am not going to think about Jamie and Caroline for the rest of the night. It's just me and my Pentax now. I heft the camera bag over my shoulder and let the front door slam behind me.

The rain has stopped, for now, but the clouds are still heavy overhead, making the world darker than I want, but I can work with it. I walk north toward Volunteer Park, the brick water tower looming out of the trees as I approach. Against the billowing clouds, the tower with its small arched windows at the top looks apocalyptic, as if it could be a stronghold against a zombie horde. I snap a picture.

Inside the tower, a metal staircase winds upward between the wall and the massive water tank. I'm breathing hard at the top, but the view is worth it. Out of the barred windows is a panoramic view in all directions. The skyscrapers of Bellevue sit across Lake Washington on the east side, the Cascade Mountains visible on sunny days, and to the southeast, Mount Rainier, if you're lucky. In middle school, we learned the Native American name for Rainier is Tahoma. Some think it originates from a word in the language spoken by the Puyallup tribe, my teacher told us then. That word means "mother of waters." The mountain isn't visible today, the clouds blanketing the sky down to the horizon, but I can feel the mass of it pulling me in, like a small sun holding the city in orbit.

On the west side, Seattle itself sprawls out, down to the Puget Sound. Across the water, I can see Bainbridge Island, and behind it, the cloud-shrouded ridges of the Olympic Mountains. Click: the mountains through the bars of the window, always so far away.

Voices on the stairs swirl up into the stillness of the observation deck. I cross to the second staircase on the other side. I don't want to be around people. I like the deck better when I have it to myself.

There's not much to shoot in the park—nothing that catches my eye, anyway—and the light is starting to fade, so I head home. Lights are on in the houses, windows framing golden worlds of people talking, making dinner, coming back from work. Our house, red brick with a wooden door, a sidewalk through a lawn to an iron gate in a low brick fence, sits at the midpoint of our street. But I don't go that way. I go down the alley, through our tiny backyard, and open the back door.

"There she is!" Dad says. He smiles at me from the stove in the kitchen. "How's our future Annie Leibovitz today?"

I roll my eyes. Mom used to call me that, and I loved it at first. But right now it feels like a weight resting in the wrong place, like a hiking backpack packed the wrong way.

"No? Ansel Adams, maybe. Diane Arbus?" He stirs the pot.

"Now you're just naming famous photographers," I call back, heading past him, through the dining room, and down the hallway to my room.

He says something, but I can't hear it, and I close the door behind me, hanging my camera bag on its hook. Off with the rain jacket and real-person clothes, on with the sweats and my favorite dark green wool sweater. The house is cold because Dad is allergic to turning on the heat, so I pull a beanie on for good measure.

My phone pings from somewhere in the pile. When I dig it out of my jacket pocket, I see the notification. It's from Jamie.

omg so i just got home from the date and guess what: we totally made out. it was right after we left the coffee shop and we were

The preview cuts off the rest of the message. For the first time in my life, I don't unlock my phone to read the rest. I leave it on the bed and walk out to the kitchen.

Dad sets me to work making the salad. He hums as he seasons the stew. It's been a long time since he's seemed this happy. Is it because he talked to Mom the other night?

He hums, and the sound makes me tense. I don't understand why he hasn't told us about the conversation. Why we haven't talked about Mom leaving since she did. What was so wrong with us that she had to leave? Maybe he thinks we can't handle it. But it's the silence that's killing me. The words swell in my throat, the questions I want to ask all crowding into each other until I think I'll explode.

"Dad?" I turn to him, still holding the bag of shredded lettuce.

He looks over at me.

The back door bangs open behind him and Garrett barges in, his huge sports bag knocking papers off the table in the nook. He curses and drops the bag, scrambling for the papers, and Dad crosses the kitchen to help him.

"How was soccer?"

Garrett shrugs, hands Dad a stack of papers. Dad backs up as Garrett slides by, the bag bumping the wall and getting caught in the doorway for a second.

"Don't forget about your essay," Dad calls after him.

"I know," Garrett says, only he shouts the last word. I'm silent, dropping lettuce into the bowl.

"Were you going to ask me something?" Dad says.

I shrug. "Nothing."

"'Nothing' means 'everything' when a teenager says it." Dad chuckles at his own line.

Now I have to say something. Of course he picks this moment to be his old self again. "Just wondering. How you are. You know. How are you?" Could I be any more awkward?

"Just fine." The spoon clinks the pot, and he starts humming again. "Thanks for asking, sweetie."

It's totally dark outside now, and the kitchen has warmed up a little from the heat of the stove. I finish the salad as fast as I can and put it on the table, heading back to my room. There are more notifications from Jamie, all of them about Caroline.

I throw the phone back on the bed without reading the texts and head out to the dining room.

CHAPTER FIVE

WHEN JAMIE KNOCKS ON THE DOOR THE NEXT DAY FOR HIS manniversary celebration, I still haven't read the texts. My chest feels like it's being squeezed by a boa constrictor. I can barely summon a smile when I let him in.

"I got the goods right here," he says, patting his backpack.

"Awesome," I say, but my voice sounds flat.

"Are you okay?"

"Just tired," I say. "I gotta grab my coat."

The nearest place we can burn anything is Golden Gardens, the beach down in the Ballard neighborhood. Getting there takes an hour and a half on the light rail and then the bus, and Jamie talks about Caroline from the moment we step out the door.

"Did you see my texts?" he asks first.

"I totally forgot to respond, I'm sorry." I grimace, hoping the expression can hide the lie in my mouth.

I never forget to respond, but Jamie doesn't question it, launching straight into a recap of the evening. After school, they'd gone to a nearby coffee shop in the University District, where they talked for two hours before leaving. The kiss happened almost right afterward, as they walked through the University of Washington campus. She'd grabbed his hand and dragged him into a nook in one of the buildings.

"It was so hot," Jamie says. "She, like, backed into the wall and pulled me against her, and then boom!" He throws his hands out. "We were making out."

"Whoa." I nod, trying to look impressed, but I just feel tense and exposed, as if I'm the one grabbed and kissed instead. I don't like the feeling, and the mental image makes my brain twitch. I push it away.

"Is this weird for you?" Jamie looks at me. We board the light rail.

I shrug. "Yeah. Kinda."

"I'm sorry. I forget you're asexual sometimes."

I shrug again, as if I can throw off that word and everything it means, or might mean, about me. "I don't know if

I'm asexual. I just don't like talking about sex. Or thinking about it. I just don't get it."

"That's pretty much the definition of 'ace.'" Jamie uses the slang term like it belongs to him, and anger washes through me. Why does he get to talk about it like that, so casual, and I'm here grasping for words?

We get off at the university and run for our connecting bus.

"We can stop talking about it if you want," Jamie says once we're seated.

"Yeah," I say. He tries to keep his face neutral, but his mouth turns down a little. "I mean, I'm really happy for you. It's just weird to hear about. Maybe later?"

"Totally." He looks out the window. "I'm just really excited. I've never had a girl like me like this before."

"What about the girlfriend you told me about, the one you had in middle school?"

"That was middle school." He drums his fingers on his thighs. "And, I don't know. She liked the girl me. Caroline likes the boy me."

Oh. Of course. I'm such an asshole. This is important to Jamie for more reasons than just the making out.

"When I started transitioning, I thought no one would

ever want to date me," he says softly. "But she does. She knows I'm trans and she doesn't care. Being trans is just part of who I am, instead of all of who I am. She gets that."

I get that, too, I want to say, but I stop myself. It's not about me. Jamie knows I'm his friend. Caroline is different. She's someone he likes romantically, and I think I can understand, now, why that matters. Why it's different. Not better—at least, I hope not. But different, and important in its own way.

"That's really cool," I say, and mean it. He smiles.

The beach is deserted when we get there, a few old couples walking the shoreline. We head for the firepit farthest from the parking lot, in case a cop rolls through and decides we're doing something wrong.

Jamie builds a perfect pyramid of kindling and newspaper pulled from his backpack, sticking a single small log in for good measure. It's cloudy, but not in the way that means rain is imminent. The sky is just regular Seattle gray. Even the Olympics are out of sight, the dark green trees on the far side of the Puget Sound disappearing into fog.

"Let's do this," Jamie says with a grin, and douses the wood in gasoline from a small canister he brought. He pulls a plastic bag and a box of matches out of his pack.

Inside the bag is a pile of bras—regular ones and sports bras. Jamie lights the match as I step back. He tosses it in, and the wood goes up in a whoosh of flame. Jamie yelps with glee. We each grab a bra, Jamie whirling his around his head before tossing it onto the fire. I drop my selection on top, and the flames gobble the material.

Pretty soon there's a hunk of melted, smoldering fabric in the pit, the fire dying down slowly. Jamie dashes down to the water and back up, racing around the iron ring and back to the water again, whooping.

"Burn, baby, burn!" he screeches. "Never again! Binders only!"

I laugh and laugh, jumping up and down, his excitement contagious.

"I can't wait till I'm eighteen," he says, smoothing his hands down his chest, flattened by the binder under his shirt. His moms' one stipulation when he came out was that he couldn't get surgery until he was legally an adult. I still wasn't sure Jamie had forgiven them for that, but he hadn't talked about it in a while. He was so angry back then, raging about how they didn't understand the torture of living in a body that didn't feel like his, how he was almost sixteen and there were surgeons who would do it with parental consent, and why couldn't they just give him that? I had to agree. His moms thought they were making the sensible choice. Surgery seemed like a big deal. And it was, but not the way they thought. I knew Jamie would be happier with a flat chest.

But they didn't back down. Eventually, especially after he started hormones, Jamie stopped talking about it as much.

He grins at me. "I want ice cream."

"Of course you do," I say.

"Full Tilt?" he asks. Our favorite ice cream shop.

"Hell yeah."

We put out the fire with his water bottle and walk back up the beach. After ice cream (Jamie: Froot Loop; me: chocolate, as usual), we bus back to my house.

In my room, Jamie does push-ups while I sort through photos, archiving them in my file cabinet by date and subject.

"I don't get it," Jamie says, rolling over onto his back for a rest.

I raise an eyebrow at him.

"That." He waves a hand at the cabinet. "Why organize if no one's going to see them?"

I shrug. "I like organizing them."

"I think you want to show people," Jamie says.

"I really don't." I focus on the pictures, labeling the backs with a Sharpie, date and subject, just in case they get mixed up.

"You've never thought about it? Not once?"

Okay. As much as Jamie's digging annoys me, he's right. Sometimes, I imagine a day in the future, when I'm in my twenties or something, wearing clothes that are way too cool for me, and I'm standing in a gallery. The gallery usually looks exactly like Mom's, just because I spent so much time there. And it's my photos lining the walls. The crowd around me is faceless, but they're all chattering, all excited—about me. The thought makes me smile.

"I knew it!"

I change the smile to a glare, but it's too late. Jamie's on his knees now, wearing the goofy grin he gets when he knows he's right.

He shakes his head. "You can't fool me."

I chuck a pillow at him and he swats it away.

"You're gonna be faaamous! You're gonna be faaa-mous!"

"Shut up!" I try to keep the glare, but I can't help laughing. "You're ridiculous."

"One day," he says, "I'll say I knew you when."

I roll my eyes, but I have to admit, I like the sound of that. Whether or not it actually happens, it's a nice thought.

::

After their date, Jamie starts sitting with Caroline at lunch every day. Sometimes I find excuses not to, but there are only so many classes I can fake having assignments for. And by that, I mean exactly three out of the six. The others I have with Jamie, and he knows what the homework is.

We used to have movie nights two or three times a week, where we tell my dad we're studying, but really we spread out our notes and books and then put a show on and watch that instead. But the first week Caroline and Jamie are together, we only have one, and he texts her the whole time.

Caroline makes zero effort to get to know me the few times I sit with them. Not that she could, when she's busy talking to Jamie, or practically eating his face off. All the girls giggle and talk louder when that happens, sneaking glances every now and then. I ignore it. It's easy to do that when Braces is talking to me. I just stare at my food and nod along with whatever she's saying.

"What's that?" she asks me one day, poking the camera bag hanging from my shoulder. She doesn't usually ask me questions, so it takes a minute to realize I'm expected to say something.

I tell her, and her eyes widen. "A film camera? Can I see?"

I shrug and open the bag, handing it to her. She takes it almost reverently. "I've never seen one of these before."

"It's not, like, a relic or anything," I say before I can stop myself. Ugh. That was rude.

She laughs, though. "Duh! I know that. It's cool. Most people our age are so obsessed with Instagram." She rolls her eyes.

I look at her for once, really look at her. Her blond hair is parted on the side today, revealing a streak of pink. Her eyes are focused on the camera, round cheeks drawn in to pursed lips as she studies it.

"You're not?" I ask.

She shakes her head. "I don't have any social media."

Suddenly I wish I could remember her name. I've never met anyone our age who doesn't have at least two, maybe three profiles. Even I still have an Instagram, although I don't use it.

"Cool." She hands it back.

"Emma!" One of the other girls joggles her shoulder. "Do you have those notes?"

She turns away, and I file her name into a corner of my brain, repeating it over and over so I won't forget again. Emma is cooler than I thought. If I'm going to be sitting here more often, I should probably get used to talking to her.

CHAPTER SIX

ON FRIDAY, JAMIE BEGS ME TO COME TO HIS BASKETBALL GAME after school, so I do. It's mostly parents in the gym. Our basketball team is good, but no sport at our school ever gets the same attention football does, even though our football team is terrible. I don't understand that at all. Maybe it's the violence, the gladiator-in-the-arena hype that gets people to the football games. Some things never change.

I sit at the top of the bleachers and find Jamie on the court in his silver home-game jersey, his ginger hair a blaze of fire as he weaves through the other team's offense. He passes the ball to a teammate, who sinks a layup. Another reason Jamie is great: He always gives the assist, hardly ever takes the shot for himself.

He's the only reason I know what an assist and a layup are—and the only reason I'd ever come to any sports game. Basketball and soccer have grown on me, thanks to him. There's an elegance to the gameplay, the teammates moving the ball like they're calculating an equation at top speed. Every basket made is like that moment in a picture when your eye, the subject, and the press of the shutter all line up.

Jamie jogs slowly toward the time-out huddle, scanning for me, and waves. I wave back. His gaze shifts and I follow it to Caroline entering the gym. He points at her, big grin on his face, and she blows him a kiss.

I watch her from my perch. Her hair is up in a long ponytail, her last name emblazoned on the back of her sweatshirt.

She turns and looks directly at me. Without thinking about it I lift a hand and wave, and she waves back, hesitantly. Then she climbs the bleachers toward me. Shit.

"Hey," she says, sitting down next to me.

I smile. Even though I want to run away. "What's up?"

She shrugs, eyes following the game. We sit in silence for a few minutes, the squeak of sneakers on linoleum and the clank of basketball on backboard masking the awkwardness. Almost. I shift in my seat, willing her to get up and leave. Even though I know that's not going to happen.

"So how long have you and Jamie been friends?" she asks finally.

"Freshman year." I watch Marc, the captain, sink a basket. "He'd just moved here from California. We sat next to each other in English. I didn't know anyone in the class either, so we started talking, and the rest is history." I smile.

"He talks about you a lot." She doesn't look at me, watching Jamie instead. "We have bio together, right?"

I remember her the other day, laughing with Tanner. Are they friends? "Yeah," I say.

She giggles. "Bones's eyebrows are unreal."

I laugh and nod. We're talking. I'm having a conversation with Caroline Summers. It's not terrible.

Our team wins by ten points and Caroline and I sit silently through most of it. I jump up as Jamie jogs up the bleachers toward us.

"You did great," I tell him, wishing for the first time ever that I had something intelligent to say about the game, something that would make me sound like I know something about basketball.

"Yeah, that three from the top of the key was so tight," Caroline says, hand on hip. They grin at each other and then their faces are smashed against each other, and I look away at the teams gathering their things up and finding their family members down on the gym floor.

"Ready?" I ask Jamie when they're done kissing. We always go out to Beth's Cafe after his games, get a big stack of pancakes and an omelette to share, draw pictures with the crayons and paper they give every customer. Drawings are plastered over every inch of the restaurant's walls.

He and Caroline look at each other.

"Oh man, I'm sorry. We were planning to go to Marc's party." He watches me, mouth turned down.

"Oh," I say.

"You should come," he says quickly. Caroline looks at him. "A bunch of people are going. It's not, like, an exclusive party or anything."

I shake my head. A party with a bunch of people I don't know? Sounds like Nightmare World.

"Come on, it'll be fun," he says. "Just this once."

I look from him to Caroline. She smiles again, lips pressed together.

"Okay," I say quietly.

"Yes!" Jamie's voice is too loud in the now-empty gym. "Caroline just got her license, so we're riding in style." He grins at both of us, and then they're trotting down the bleachers hand in hand. I'm following them like I'm in someone else's body, someone who goes to basketball after-parties, someone who hangs out with people besides Jamie. Just this once.

We crawl out of the parking lot in Caroline's sedan, bumper to bumper with the other cars. Heat blasts from the vents, fogging up the windows. I wipe clear an opening with my hand and lean my head against the glass, looking up at the clear night sky, the bare branches of the trees. Jamie and Caroline sing along to the radio, but I don't know the words.

The party is loud. We hear it through the closed windows of Caroline's station wagon from the curb when we arrive. When we get out, the bass unfurls like a carpet from the open door. Inside, I can see people packed in all the way down the hall. I wish I could teleport home. Instead, I trail Jamie and Caroline as they walk up to the house.

It's a massive Craftsman house, except everything is too big. That's how you know it's new and not an original Craftsman. That's how you know the owner is rich. Apparently, Marc is hosting because his parents are out of town. What is this, a classic teen movie? I can feel my eyeballs straining from the effort of not rolling.

In the living room, there's a table with nine kinds of unidentifiable punch and Top 40 music playing at full volume, the bass vibrating in my chest. The song is a total throwback: "I Gotta Feeling" by the Black Eyed Peas. I imagine a new refrain in the same tune: "I don't wanna beee here!" Guaranteed banger.

I'm still behind Jamie and Caroline like the pointless caboose on their train of CandyGram love. In the kitchen, Jamie finds what he's looking for: beer. He cracks open two and hands one to Caroline, offering me the other. I shake my head. He shrugs and chugs it while Caroline claps her hands, urging him on.

Marc comes in, still wearing his jersey. He's tall, towering over us, an easy smile turning his cheeks pink under his warm brown skin. His hair is black and curly on top, faded at the sides, with a perfect straight line buzzed into one side. He's the kind of guy everyone feels like they're friends with, even if they aren't.

"What's up, my dude?" He and Jamie bump fists. "You were all over the assists tonight." Jamie blushes, waves a hand like it's nothing. "You must be Caroline." Marc holds out a hand and Caroline shakes it, smiling. "Jamie won't shut up about you."

"Aww!" She pushes Jamie's shoulder.

Marc turns to me with that big grin. "I don't think we've met."

"I'm Arden Grey," I say. "I'm Jamie's best friend."

Marc reaches over and grabs a beer, tossing it to me, and I catch it reflexively. He cracks one of his own. "Marc Davis. Nice to meet you. Thanks for coming, y'all." He slides out of the conversation and into the living room. I stare at the beer in my hand. I've had a few sips of beer and wine before, at home when my parents had some with dinner, but never enough to get drunk. I pop the tab and take a sip. Jamie and Caroline laugh as I stick my tongue out.

"It's an acquired taste," Caroline says, as if she's drunk a lot of beers. Maybe she has. I've heard stories about the boys' soccer team and their parties from Jamie. The girls' team is probably the same.

An hour later, Jamie and Caroline are drunk and grinding on each other in the living room. I stand against the wall, looking everywhere but at them. I imagine I'm watching a movie, the same teen classic. I guess that makes me the loser. Or the shy one who will come out of her shell at the end. I'm not Sandy though, and this isn't *Grease*. I wouldn't wear a bodysuit if my life depended on it.

I finished my beer, even though I hated every second of it, and now my body feels warm, my head fuzzy. Time moves slower.

"Arden Grey." Marc materializes next to me. "Wanna dance?" Without thinking I wrinkle my nose and he holds up his hands. "Sorry, did I say something wrong?"

I shake my head. "No. I just don't dance."

"You don't, or you're just scared to?" He starts moving, swaying his shoulders back and forth, smiling at me. Why is he paying attention to me? I'm nobody. Jamie has already forgotten about me. I look at him and Caroline, their mouths open, hands all over each other. Marc follows my stare. "Oh, I see."

See what? Oh shit. "No, no," I say. "It's not like that. I don't like Jamie that way."

"Well, if you're not waiting on anyone . . ." Marc says.

"I'm not interested."

"You don't have to be interested in anyone to dance. I'm not," he says.

I laugh before I can stop myself.

"What?" He tilts his head, half-smiling.

"It's just . . ." I gesture at him. The beer must be hitting me, because I'm being way more honest than normal. "You're the senior homecoming king. The captain of the basketball team. You must have girls all over you. If you're straight. I guess you could be gay. Or bi." Oh my god, I need to stop talking.

The bass pauses as the song changes, something faster. He shakes his head, looking away into the crowd. "I'm not anything."

I look at him then, really look at him. His hands clasp together, fingers cracking knuckles back and forth. Diamond studs sparkle in his ears. "What do you mean?"

He shrugs. "Never mind. I'm gonna get another beer."

Just like that, I'm alone again, but his words are ringing in my ears. Marc Davis isn't anything? Isn't straight, gay, or bi? Isn't interested in anyone? What does that mean?

I stew on that for an hour, until Caroline finally sobers up enough to drive. She's still a little tipsy, and I think about protesting for a minute, but neither Jamie nor I have our licenses and it's too late to catch the bus. I sit in the backseat, clutching the safety handle above the door while Jamie nuzzles her neck at the red lights.

"Text me when you get home," I tell him when they drop me off.

"It's fine, Arden," Caroline says, her voice brittle, but Jamie throws a thumbs-up and a big grin my way.

The house is dark, Dad and Garrett asleep. I make my-self a piece of toast and go up to my room. It's nice that Dad trusts me, I guess. Right now, I wish he trusted me less. I want to talk to him.

I eat the toast and try to sleep, but I can't. The beer has worn off and now I'm just awake, replaying the night over and over in my mind. The happy crowd at the party; Marc's words, resigned but certain; Jamie and Caroline wound together like snakes. Ugh.

The bed is too warm, the covers too close. I turn on the lamp and slide onto the floor, finding my phone and put-ting in my earbuds. The screen scrolls under my finger-tips, song after song, until I find the right one.

Modest Mouse fills my ears. My chest feels hollow and full at the same time, like something sharp is trying to push its way out. I want to cry, but I can't, and thoughts crowd in, everything bad wanting to be heard. I turn up the volume until the song hurts my ears. It's almost enough to drown out everything else.

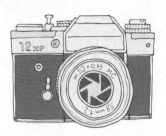

CHAPTER SEVEN

CAROLINE IS GONE ON TUESDAY FOR A FIELD TRIP, AND FOR THE first time in a week and half, it's just me and Jamie for lunch. He jumps to his feet when I find him in the hallway across from his locker.

"Check this out." He shoves a flyer at me. "It was on the bulletin board in the art hallway."

The flyer is covered in blocky shapes and bright hues, letters in purple spelling out a name: Riot Gallery. "Call for artists," reads the flyer. "We are a collective of photographers based in and around Seattle. Riot Gallery is our answer to the commercialization of photography. We want to bring back the experience of a photo as art, as emotion without a profit margin, as an image worth a thousand words. For our gallery opening, we are curating half the photos and seeking submissions for the rest of the exhibit. Theme: Riot! A riot opens a space, explodes social norms, interrupts business as usual. A riot is a reclaiming, a re-invention, a revolution. A riot can be quiet or loud, colorful or stark, subtle or in-your-face. Send us your best. We expect nothing less."

Below that, submission details. Jamie wears a wide smile like he already knows what he wants me to say, and my eyes narrow. "I'm not submitting."

His shoulders drop, hands thrown upward. "Come on! Why not?"

"My photos are just for me." I looked down at the flyer. "Besides, there's no way they'll pick me. I'm just some random kid with a camera. I'm not a professional or anything."

"Then why would they put their call on a bulletin board at a school?" Jamie crosses his arms.

I cross mine and we lock eyes.

"You'll have to let someone see eventually," he says.

"No, I won't." I sound ridiculous and petty and I know it. I stare at the call for artists again. I already know what photo I would submit. I look up at Jamie. He smirks. He knows he's won. "Fine."

"Yes!" He pumps a fist. "I can't wait to go to the opening."

"I haven't even submitted yet!"

"Whatever. They'll pick you."

The bell rings and I go to class, flyer still in my hand. I fold it as small as I can and shove it into my jacket pocket, turning it over in my fingers like a charm.

∷▪▪▪∷

I talk more at lunch now, to Emma (who I've finally stopped calling Braces in my head), about the books we're reading, the shows we're watching, our favorite characters and celebrities. I learn that she's bisexual, but she's never dated anyone either, like me. Sometimes, we share a sidelong glance when Jamie and Caroline are kissing, and it warms me, like I'm not the only one who finds their public makeouts bizarre. Like, sure, to each their own. But I can't imagine a universe in which it's comfortable to let people stare at you while you have your tongue in someone else's mouth.

Jamie seems to love it, though. All his texts now are about Caroline, what they're talking about, how he feels, but never what they're doing physically. Maybe he still remembers the day we burned his bras, and what I said then, and I'm relieved. Both because I don't have to hear any more details, and because I don't have to have that conversation with him again.

The week after Jamie gives me the call for artists, I sit in my chair staring at the submission page on their website. I've already written a bio and an artist statement, but there's one last thing I need to do.

Hey so I'm working on that gallery submission and I have a question. I send the text and wait for Jamie's reply.

For once, I don't have to wait forever for a response. Lately, if it's not Caroline-related, the wait between texts stretches out longer and longer. But not this time. **YESSSS. What's up?**

Can I use that photo of you doing your shot?

The moment I read the call, I thought of that picture, the keeper from that color roll. It's a perfect fit with how they defined a riot: As a reclaiming. A reinvention. Subtle, or in your face. Jamie's transition is all of that. It's so his, so private, the changes barely noticeable sometimes, like the tiny hairs he showed me, growing on his cheeks; other times obvious, like the way his voice cracked and dropped an octave during an oral presentation. He's reclaiming himself, who he is and always was. Reinventing the way others see him.

My phone pings. **Omg totally. My face in a gallery...**
we're both gonna be famous

Lol sure. I can't help it. I'm smiling at my phone. For a
minute, it almost feels like it did before Caroline.

I attach a scan of the photo and hit send on my submission to Riot Gallery, my heart pounding as the confirmation screen pops up. Maybe I'll know by Friday, and Jamie
and I can celebrate. We're finally having a movie night, the
first one in weeks.

I want to talk to him about it, sometimes. How it feels
more and more like he'd rather be with Caroline than me.
How it sucks that we don't text or hang out the way we used
to. But then he does something that makes me remember
how great our friendship is, and I don't say anything. It's
probably better not to. I don't want to seem weird or pos-
sessive. And it won't be this way forever. At least, I hope it
won't.

On Friday, I wait for Jamie at my locker, fiddling with my
phone. I feel strange, almost nervous, which makes no
sense. This is Jamie. Yeah, we haven't hung out just the
two of us in a while, but it's not like we had a fight.

The hall clears out slowly, until I'm the only one left, the banks of lockers stretching away toward the doors to the parking lot. I swivel the other way, but there's no one. Around the corner, a locker bangs shut and footsteps trail away, until the hall is silent again.

I wait for five more minutes, and then walk slowly toward the parking lot. Passing the gym, I hear the screech of sneakers and basketballs bouncing, and I stop. Maybe Jamie got caught up after P.E.

But there's just a few guys in the gym shooting baskets, Jamie's red hair nowhere in sight. One of them is Marc. He catches a shot coming off the backboard, and as he dribbles back toward the gym doors, he sees me.

He stops, pointing a finger at me across the court. "Arden Grey. How's it going?"

"Fine," I say. "Have you seen Jamie?"

He laughs. "Oh yeah. He was leaving with his girl when we got in here."

All the blood in my veins freezes. "Did he say where he was going?"

Marc shrugs. "Sorry, no idea."

"Okay, thanks." I turn to go, then turn back when Marc calls my name again.

He jogs up to me and stands, tossing the ball hand to hand, biting his lip. "Hey. About the party. I hope I didn't make things awkward."

I shake my head. Up close, the facade of bravado is gone, the veil of cool dropped. He shifts from foot to foot, spinning the ball on one finger.

"It's really okay," I say, and he nods. "How do you do that?" I point at the ball, rotating at perfect speed on his fingertip.

He looks at it as if noticing it for the first time, and he moves his hand, palming the ball and bringing it to his side. "I don't know. It's easy." He grins at me, but not the team captain–smooth grin. It's a real grin, like he's a little kid all of a sudden. "I can show you sometime."

"Sure." I don't know why, but I'm smiling, too. Charm or no charm, Marc still has that vibe, like he'd be the greatest friend ever. I have no interest in basketball, but being able to spin one on my finger would be pretty cool.

"Marc!" One of the guys yells from the hoop. "Two on two!"

He nods at me, still grinning, and jogs away to join them. I turn around again and walk out of the gym, reality returning. Out of Marc's glow, the ice forms again inside my body. Jamie left with Caroline.

In the parking lot, I scan for her car. It's not hard, since almost everyone is gone.

And so is she. The sedan is nowhere in sight.

Jamie stood me up.

CHAPTER EIGHT

I STAND IN THE PARKING LOT FOR A FEW MINUTES, TRYING NOT to cry. I don't know if I should be as upset as I am, if I'm allowed to feel this betrayed—but I do. Barely three weeks of dating Caroline, and Jamie's already forgetting me. Is this what happens when people date? If it is, I don't want any part of it. I thought I was important to Jamie. But not as important as someone he can make out with. Someone he barely knew a month ago.

Eventually, I walk to the bus and ride home in a daze, until I'm in my room. No one's home, and I'm relieved. I shut my door and lie down on my bed, and then the tears come.

I haven't cried since Mom left us, but now it all comes pouring out, a flood, and I can't stop it. My whole body shakes, and I howl into my pillow. I hate Caroline. I hate her. I knew there was a reason why I wasn't excited about her dating Jamie, and I was right. She doesn't care about getting to know me, or about Jamie's life outside her. She wants him all to herself.

I think of Dad in his room, and the ragged edges of his voice. *What about the kids?*

What about us, Mom? I cry harder, soaking the pillow.

"Arden?" Dad's voice comes through my door. I stop crying. "I heard you just now. Is everything okay?"

"No!" I yell. Of course it isn't okay. How can he even ask that?

"Can I come in?"

I stare at the wall. I don't know if I want him to come in or not. The decision feels too hard to make right now.

"I'm coming in. Yell if you want me not to." The knob turns, and his footsteps cross the floor. I feel a weight settling onto the bed behind me. I curl up and he puts a hand on my shoulder. "What's going on?"

"Jamie."

He hmmms. "What about Jamie?"

Unlike Mom, he doesn't ask me about my feelings for Jamie, like there should be something other than friendship between us. "He ditched me."

"Ouch." He squeezes my shoulder.

"For his new girlfriend." The words roll twisted and bitter off my tongue.

"I'm so sorry, honey."

"I don't get it. How can you just forget you're supposed to hang out with your best friend?" I reach out and push my fingers against the wall, one at a time.

Dad is silent for a moment. "Jamie's feeling a lot of new things right now, I'd imagine. When you're attracted to someone, your judgment goes out the window sometimes."

"Like you and Mom." I know I'm being mean, but it feels good somehow. Like I can finally be mad at her, say what I could never say when she was around.

Dad lets out a breath. "Your mom and I . . ." His hand leaves my shoulder and I roll onto my back to look at him. He rubs his face, then drops his hands into his lap, clasping them as he stares out the window. "It's complicated."

"Then why did she leave?" The tears surge up and I wipe them away.

"I don't know." He looks at me. "I don't know if she even knows. She's always been restless. A perfectionist. She has high expectations, and she wants her life to meet them."

"And we didn't." I cross my arms.

"That's not what I meant," he replies. I turn my face away and he gently grasps my chin, pulling me back to look at him. "Arden. You and Garrett didn't do anything wrong. This is about her, okay? Me and her."

I don't understand how that's different or what it means, but I nod anyway. He holds my gaze for a minute, and I notice for the first time how many new lines there are on his face, deep ones in his forehead, like dry canyons in miniature.

"You should talk to Jamie." He pats my shoulder and stands up.

I shrug.

"Give him the benefit of the doubt. He's been your best friend a lot longer than he's been Caroline's boyfriend. He'd want to know if he hurt your feelings."

"Okay."

"Thatagirl." He smiles and I manage a small one back, even though it doesn't feel real.

When he leaves, I check my phone. No new messages. I want to throw it across the room, but I make myself unlock it and type out a message to Jamie.

hey what happened? thought we were hanging tonight. i'm at home if you wanna come over

I hit send and toss it onto the carpet. Come on, Jamie. Don't let me down.

Please don't let me down.

The morning comes, and still no text from Jamie. I lie in bed, feeling like I haven't slept at all, laptop still open next to my pillow. I fell asleep watching Netflix last night, trying to distract myself from the ache in my chest.

I stare at my phone, willing it to ping. Finally, I give in and pick it up, dialing Jamie's number. We almost never talk on the phone. When we do, it's only because we have to: a last-minute confirmation of plans, or an emergency. Like the night he came out to his moms and needed moral support right before he did it. Or any one of the times Mom said something to me, something so awful I couldn't brush it off. Jamie was the only person I could tell about the way she made me feel.

The phone rings, and he picks up.

"Hey," he says, the cheerfulness too much.

I meant to ask casually, but it all goes away at the sound of his voice. "What happened last night?" I sound like I'm accusing him, but I don't care. He has no right to act like there's nothing wrong.

"I'm so, so, so, so sorry," he says. "I totally, oh man. I just. I forgot."

I knew he had, but the word still hits me in the chest like a punch. "Marc said you left with Caroline."

"Yeah. Shit." His voice sounds heavy. "She met me after P.E., and we were talking, and I don't know. I was so caught up, I left with her. By the time I saw your text, we were making out. It just seemed awkward to leave. And when I mentioned it later, she didn't want me to go."

Later. After what? I don't want to think about that. "And that's it? Just because she doesn't want you to go, you don't?"

He doesn't say anything.

"We had plans, Jamie. I thought I was your best friend."

"She's my girlfriend, Arden."

The word rolls off his tongue as if it's a get-out-of-jail-free card. "You've barely known her a month!" My voice is raised, but I don't care.

"You don't get it," he says, and he's talking louder, too, voice cracking.

"What's that supposed to mean?" I ask, even though I know.

"Why are you acting like this?"

"Like what?" I can barely force the words out. Jamie sounds angry now, and he's never been angry at me.

"You're acting super jealous. We're not dating, Arden. We're just friends." I want to stop him, tell him I know that, and it doesn't make me less important than Caroline, but he barrels on. "You've been acting weird ever since I started seeing Caroline. You didn't even try to like her. I know it's been tough since your mom left, but I can't be your only friend. I'm tired of being your only friend."

"You're not my only friend," I say, but I know he's right. The world is fuzzing out around me, every particle in my body focused on his voice seething through the phone speaker.

"I deserve to have a life, too."

"I know." My voice is tiny now.

"Stop doing that!"

"What am I doing?" I draw my knees up, confusion swirling in my brain.

"You're shrinking like you do whenever anyone is upset with you," he says, and his voice is quieter now. "I can hear it in your voice."

"What are you talking about?"

A long sigh echoes through the phone. "When people are mad at you, or mad near you, you get smaller. Your voice gets quiet and you try to, I don't know. Shrink yourself."

I look down at my body, knees up to my chest, free arm wrapped around them, hugging myself tightly. I'd never noticed it before. "Why?"

"I don't know."

"Please don't be mad at me."

"I'm . . ." He trails off. "I know I fucked up. I should have left Caroline's house as soon as I realized. She just . . . she really didn't want me to go. She got all . . . I don't know. She said she thought you were into me. Trying to steal me from her."

"What?" I'm so surprised I laugh out loud. "You and I were friends first. How can I steal you from her?"

"I know. I think that's why." He sighs. "She's jealous."

"Then why did you accuse me of being the jealous one?" I slide onto the carpet and lie down, propping my heels on the edge of the bed.

"Well, you kind of are. Not in the romantic sense," he says hastily. "I know it's not like that. But you're like . . . friend-jealous."

I don't say anything, just stare at the ceiling. Am I? I guess I am. I'm worried Caroline is going to take Jamie away from me, just the way she's apparently worrying about me doing the same thing. But the difference is, she actually is. We were fine before she showed up. He never forgot me before she showed up. He's been spending all his time with her. What reason does she have to be jealous? She hasn't tried to get to know me, either.

You don't get it. Jamie's words echo in my head. I know what he means: I don't understand romance, sex, the way it makes people feel, the way it makes them act. Except I do. I've spent my whole life watching other people freak out over attractive celebrities, watched countless romcoms where people fall in love and have sex after a single glance, seen my parents fight one day and then seem completely fine the next. It just never seemed realistic, or healthy, or fun to me. Just exhausting. And I've never felt that way, never been swept off my feet or wanted to rip someone's clothes off the moment I met them.

So maybe in that sense, I don't get it. But I see it.

"Arden?"

"Yeah?"

"Are we cool?"

I don't know if we are. Everything we said hangs in the air, like bubbles waiting to pop. *I can't be your only friend. I'm tired of being your only friend.* But I don't know what to say about that, and I don't think I can handle an explanation from him. So I just close my eyes and nod. "We're cool."

After he hangs up, I lie there for a long time, eyes unfocused, replaying the conversation over and over. It hurts every time, like a dull knife stabbing me in the heart. Or the back. What if Jamie leaves me, too? The thought is an abyss, and I pull back from it. That's not going to happen. He wouldn't do that. We're best friends.

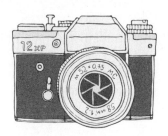

CHAPTER NINE

WALKING INTO SCHOOL ON MONDAY FEELS LIKE WALKING INTO
a gunfight. The hallway stretches out like the main streets
of the small towns in all the Westerns Jamie and I spent
one summer watching, and I'm waiting for the moment
I see Caroline, or Jamie, or both of them together. Jamie
and I are cool, supposedly. We talked it out. But the phone
call didn't feel like enough, and Jamie's words still hang
over me like gun smoke.

I keep my head down, not looking at anyone, and get
from my locker to my first class. Safe. I slide into my seat.
At least I don't have this period with Jamie.

As second period approaches, my guts twist and churn.
I can't stop looking at the clock. When the bell rings, I drag
myself out.

I don't want to feel this way about Jamie. But when I
walk into our second-period class, and see him sitting

there, in front of my seat like always, and he looks up and sees me, I stop short. He waves, an awkward raise of one hand, and I force my feet forward, one at a time, until I sit down behind him.

He turns around and doesn't say anything. People shuffle in, high-fiving, talking about the assignment, drawing on the whiteboard while the teacher looks on with a tolerant smile. The pressure builds until I can't stand it.

"This is awkward," I mumble, and Jamie snorts.

"Yeah." He nods. "I'm sorry. I was an asshole."

I can't help smiling. This is the Jamie I know. "Yeah, you were."

"Are we really cool?" His forehead wrinkles as he watches me.

I nod, and I know it's true this time. Jamie was right: he is my only friend. But I'm okay with that. He's the best friend anyone could have. I don't need other friends. I talk to other people—Marc, Emma, Dad—but Jamie is the person I confide in. There's nothing wrong with that.

Jamie grins. "Good."

That whole week, the first week of December, the temperatures drop into the low forties, taunting us with the possibility of snow but never delivering. The rain falls, icy and unrelenting. On Thursday, I step out of the bus and into a puddle, the water soaking through my Vans in seconds. Squeaking through the halls, I wiggle my toes, trying to keep them warm, until I get to a bathroom. Inside, I take my shoes off and wring my socks out in the sink, then hold them under the hand dryer. Some tiny freshman girls stand giggling at the mirror, sneaking glances at me. I imagine them spreading the story later. I'll become known as the Weird Bathroom Junior.

Whatever. The bell rings and they dash out. I tug the damp socks back on, force my feet into my shoes, and squeak my way to first period.

A text from Jamie lets me know he's home sick. I feel bad for him, but relieved, too; I'm off the hook for lunchtime. When it finally comes, I grab my sandwich from my locker and head for the library. Emma might notice I'm gone, but I doubt Caroline will.

The library is quiet, a few other kids eating and studying at tables, a bunch of people at the computers pretending to study while trying to get around the parental controls so they can play games. I find a table in the back, near the nonfiction, grab a book of Cindy Sherman's photos off the shelf, and settle in.

Mom never liked Cindy Sherman's work. She thought it was too pop, too garish, too self-involved. But that's why I like it. Cindy isn't afraid to put herself in front of the camera, and when she does, she turns herself into someone else. My favorites of her works are her *Untitled Film Stills*, black-and-white photographs, and in each one she poses: on a street, in a kitchen, in front of a mirror, as a stereotype of a woman from an old movie. But reenacted. Reinterpreted. As if by putting herself in the role, she's asking it a question, asking the woman a question: Who were you? Who did you want to be?

I flip through the huge book of my other favorite series of hers, *Centerfolds*. Large-format pictures in bright, translucent color film; Cindy splayed across a bed or curled on a couch, face almost expressionless. Sometimes, when I lie on the floor of my room, I imagine I'm in one of her photographs.

Someone passes me and I look up, catching the back of Caroline's sweatshirt as she stops a few shelves over. She has to have seen me, but she doesn't say anything. Should

I say something? I sit there a moment too long, staring at her, and then she looks back. Right at me.

"Arden! Hi." She smiles too wide. "I didn't even see you there."

"Surprise." I shrug, trying to keep my voice light. Her eyes shift to the shelf and back to me.

"How are you?" she asks, fingers combing the books. She's looking at the World War II section, which means she also has Ms. Maldonado for history.

"Fine." There's a drift of something underneath her voice. And probably under mine, if I'm being honest. It's strange to sit here and talk to her like nothing happened, like I don't know what Jamie told me, that she's jealous of me. In the moment, when he said it, it seemed so ridiculous. But now, with her standing right in front of me, I want to take the knife and twist it in. Just a little further. "Bummer that Jamie's sick," I say, as casually as I can.

Her fingers stop moving for a second. "He's sick?" She pulls a book out, looks at the blurb on the inside.

I watch her. So Jamie didn't tell her. I don't know what that means, but I know she isn't happy about it. "Yeah, he texted me this morning. We talk a lot."

She smiles, but it looks stiff. "Your little friendship is so cute."

"We've been best friends a long time," I say. "He always texts me when something's up." I'm really digging the knife in now, and it's not subtle, but I don't care.

She claps the book shut. The smile is gone when she looks at me, her eyes cold. But her voice, when she speaks, is breezy. "That's so nice of him." As if he's doing me a favor. I open my mouth, but she beats me to it. "See you later."

And just like that, she's gone, up to the front desk, and then out the door with the book in her hand, never once glancing back. I look down at the photograph on the page in front of me. Cindy's curled on a couch in a purple dress, staring at an old phone, the kind with a touch pad on its white body and a receiver sitting on top, a cord winding down and out of the frame. The light is golden and comes from above, hitting her jawline and shoulder, as if it's late evening and she's waiting. The picture makes me feel lonely, and I shut the book. I don't know why I tried to mess with Caroline, and all of a sudden it just feels stupid, like a big game with rules I barely know, and an ending where no one wins.

I'm still thinking about Caroline when I get home, and the more I do, the angrier I feel. How dare she talk down to me, minimize my friendship with Jamie? I sit at the kitchen counter, eating peanut butter out of the jar, and text him.

Caroline was weird to me today

Seconds go by, then minutes. No response.

"That's disgusting," Garrett says behind me, and I start so hard I almost fall off the stool. He snickers.

"What?" I ask, pretending like nothing happened. He points to the peanut butter jar, then grabs the orange juice carton from the fridge, swigging straight from it.

"Are you serious?" I roll my eyes at him.

"Hey, my mouth isn't touching this," he says, and aims another stream of juice down his throat. "You're literally scooping your germs into that jar."

"Since when have you cared about germs?"

"I don't." He strolls out. It takes all my willpower not to wing the jar after him.

Ping. I look at my phone.

we just got done talking, Jamie says. why did you tell her i was sick? she was really upset with me.

I frown. how was i supposed to know you didn't tell her?

ugh you're right, i'm sorry. it just wasn't fun trying to explain to her that i forgot.

so what? everyone forgets things sometimes. I think of my reaction to him standing me up. Am I really in a position to say that? But this is different. It's not like he flaked on her and hung out with someone else. He just forgot to text her.

idk. it's complicated.

I don't see how it's complicated, but I don't know what to say to that. how are you feeling?

better. i've been throwing up all day. i'm gonna be out tomorrow too. hey, what did you mean she was weird to you?

idk. i was in the library at lunch and she came in and pretended not to see me? and then after i told her you were out, she got all condescending about our friendship. or our "little friendship," as she called it. 🙁

that IS weird. that doesn't sound like something caroline would say

i mean, i was there. she did. I'm starting to feel annoyed now. It's like Caroline exists in this vacuum of holiness for Jamie, like she can do no wrong. It makes me think of Mom, how she would get snippy and distant with Dad for no reason, and they'd disappear into their room for hours, talking in voices too quiet for us to hear the words, but loud enough to feel the tension stretching through the house like a tightrope. Then they'd come out, finally, and

Mom would be all smiles, like nothing had ever happened, Dad trailing behind her like a puppy. It always felt weird to me. Just like this does.

i'm sorry, Jamie says. i'll talk to her

You don't have to do that, I say. Because even though I want him to, I know it won't help. She'll just hate me even more. Plus, it'll be so awkward, like I just went and tattled to Jamie. Good job not seeming jealous, Arden. I press my forehead into my hands.

Jamie doesn't respond, and I leave my phone face-down on the counter, putting the peanut butter back and wandering into the living room. Garrett's there, playing video games again, and for a minute I want to join him, shoot zombies, lose myself in the on-screen bloodbath.

"Why are you staring at me?" Garrett doesn't look up.

"God, Garrett. I can't look at you for one second?" My voice snaps out like a whip and his head jerks up.

"What's your problem?" He throws down the controller.

"I wouldn't have one if you weren't such an asshole."

He comes at me, shoving me, and I shove him back as hard as I can. He stumbles, falling onto the couch.

"What the hell is going on?" Dad yells behind us, and we both freeze. He stomps in from the kitchen and stands between us. "Garrett, we're going to talk. Arden, go to your room."

I'm frozen, my insides falling into themselves. I've never heard Dad shout like that before. He looks at me, and his face softens. "Arden. Now, please."

I turn and walk to my room as fast as I can, slamming the door behind me. I don't want to be anywhere near Garrett. I want to be far away from here. I want everything to stop and go back to the way it was before. Mom leaving doesn't give Garrett the right to be a jerk. She left me, too, and I'm not acting out. I'm fine.

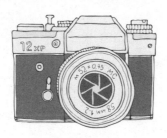

CHAPTER TEN

THE WEEKEND IS TENSE. GARRETT REFUSED TO APOLOGIZE TO me, so Dad grounded him, except for soccer practice and school. Garrett gives me the silent treatment—not that I care.

On Sunday, I open my email and there's a name I've never seen before. Natalia May. *Welcome to the Riot,* reads the subject line. I click on it after a moment of hesitation. Is it spam?

But it's not. It's from the gallery. Riot Gallery. About the show. *Congratulations, Arden!* reads the greeting, and my heart starts to pound. *We are pleased to accept your submission for our opening show.*

I read the rest in a blur, then read it again. They picked me. They thought my photo was *moving,* and *a brilliant use of angle and color,* and holy shit. They. Picked. Me.

"Oh my god." I stand straight up from my desk, staring at the photo of Hayley Kiyoko. She smirks back, as if to say, You did it, babe. I grab my phone and dial Jamie's number, and as it rings I remember we haven't texted since Thursday night. I pull the phone away from my cheek to hang up and then I hear his voice.

I put the phone back to my ear.

"Arden?" he repeats. "What's up?"

"I got in," I say, pushing past the awkwardness.

"Got in where?"

"The show! The gallery! Riot Gallery picked my photo!" The excitement balloons again, carrying my voice higher and louder.

"Holy fuck! Yes! I knew they'd pick you!" he shouts. Like nothing's wrong. And maybe nothing is wrong. Maybe it's all in my head. I laugh wildly, jumping around my room now, onto my bed, and he whoops on the other end.

"We need to celebrate," he says. "Dick's? Thirty minutes?"

"Fuck yeah," I say, and we hang up.

Dick's Drive-In sits down on Broadway, the main street through my neighborhood. Capitol Hill. The gayborhood. Or at least, it used to be, until Amazon moved to town and all the young, hip tech workers decided they wanted to live here and drove out anyone who couldn't afford it. That's what Dad always says, anyway. He used to tell me stories about living on the Hill in the eighties, going to gay bars with his drag queen friends, how he paid $250 a month for a studio. You can pay six times that much now, if you're lucky.

Even with the changes, Capitol Hill is still the place where the gay people and the weirdos go, at least in my opinion. I know I don't look weird on the outside, but I feel weird on the inside, and when I walk down Broadway, I feel at home.

I can smell the fries cooking a block away. Dick's is mobbed, but it always is now—whether it's a Friday night, suburban bros and their girlfriends grabbing a burger before they hit the club, or a day like today, all the tourist families lined up for milkshakes. I give a dollar to the busker playing on the sidewalk and wait for Jamie.

He comes from the same direction as me, but off the bus from the Madison Valley neighborhood east of Capitol Hill. He waves at me through the crowd, and my heart starts thumping. We were okay on the phone; what about when we're face-to-face? I wonder if I should say something about Caroline again, find out for sure whether he believes me that she said what she said.

I open my mouth, but he goes straight for the hug, squeezing me tight, and I hug him back. He smiles when he pulls away. "We haven't hung out in so long."

I smile. "I know, right?" Of course I know.

"I'm starving. Let's get some Dick's," he says with heavy innuendo, wiggling his eyebrows, and I laugh. Those jokes never get old, even though they still make me a little uncomfortable.

The line goes fast and pretty soon we're perched on a bench in Cal Anderson Park a few blocks south, mouths full of burgers and greasy fries. Our breath frosts the air. I'm cold, but not too cold in my thick down jacket. It's one of those sunny early winter days, crisp and clear.

"I talked to Caroline," Jamie says out of nowhere. I take a swig of my milkshake. "She said she didn't say that."

Brain freeze. I press my fingers to my forehead. "I literally heard her. She called it our 'little friendship.'" The ache recedes. He's still toying with a fry, swirling it through the ketchup in different patterns. "Jamie. You believe me."

He sighs. "Of course I do."

The silence is like ice spreading between us, freezing the surface of a lake in which we're both standing. I can't move.

"Are you sure you didn't mishear her?" he says.

"I did not mishear her." I run it through my mind again. Her at the bookshelf, freezing as I tell her Jamie is sick. That we talk a lot. How she didn't even look at me as she replied, like I was a mosquito she was trying to ignore. *Your little friendship is so cute.* She did say it quietly. Maybe she said a different word and I mistook it for *little*.

No. No. I know that's what she said. I know it in my heart. But now my brain isn't so sure. Jamie waits, still tracing his fry through the ketchup. "I don't know," I say finally. "I don't think I did. I guess it's possible." The ice hardens around my knees, freezing me limb by limb.

"She's just not like that," Jamie says. Soft, almost pleading. "It really hurt her feelings that you thought she said that. She likes you, Arden. She said she's just intimidated by you. You're my best friend, and she barely knows you."

"She hasn't tried to get to know me, either," I say. I feel sick.

"I know." Jamie looks out across the park. A dog chases a ball across the still-frosty grass. "Maybe we could all hang out. I don't want to make you the third wheel. But like, you, me, her, and maybe Emma? I noticed you've been talking at lunch."

I don't want to do this. "Sure," I say.

"Awesome." He glances at me finally, smiling, but not his usual big grin. This smile is tentative, half-formed, like he's not sure how he feels. But he's always been sure. That's one of the things I love about him. When I'm drowning in uncertainty, he's always there to tell me it's going to be fine, or that my photos are great, or that Mom shouldn't have said whatever she said to me. But now we're both frozen, the ice holding us apart.

"Maybe we can hit Pike Place Market." He pops the fry into his mouth. "Caroline's never been."

"Sounds good."

And that's the way we talk for the rest of our hangout. Him speculating, imagining. Me with robot responses. He doesn't notice, or at least, he doesn't say anything about it. Either way, the effect is the same.

⁘⁘⁘

I eat in the library every day for lunch the next week. I know I should be in the lunchroom with Jamie and Caroline and the rest of them. I should be trying to get to know Caroline. But the truth is, I don't want to. I keep replaying our conversation in my head. I know she called it *your little friendship*. I know she did. But every time I decide to tell Jamie that, the words stick in my brain like peanut butter, slow and heavy, gumming up my thoughts. I'm stupid to focus on it, anyway. It was one sentence. One word. And I wasn't very nice either. I don't know why I'm making such a big deal out of it.

Essay research, I tell Jamie every day. And every day he nods, widening his eyes, all sympathy and wow and Maldonado doesn't fuck around. He doesn't have her for history, and he knows I like research. It's true, and that's what makes it such an effective lie.

I do actually work on the essay. I pull books off the shelves and find relevant passages and snap pics of them on my phone for later; I write an outline detailing my topic. I'm not just eating alone and staring out the window. But sometimes I do. I try to make my mind blank and focus on the bare branches of the trees outside, the raindrops caught on the smooth bark, or the bright colors of the cars in the student parking lot, or the custodian ambling down toward his office by the gym.

It doesn't work. I think of Garrett, still not speaking to me; of my texts with Jamie slowed to a trickle; of Caroline Caroline Caroline saying *little friendship little friendship little friendship* over and over, her voice soft and mocking. Of Mom, somewhere in San Francisco. I haven't heard Dad talking to her since that night in his room, and she hasn't contacted me. And if she hasn't talked to me, she definitely isn't talking to Garrett.

I'd heard Mom and Garrett fighting once, in his room. She spoke in that cool tone she used when she was mad and he was yelling back. About homework, video games. *You will not leave this room until you are done. Fuck you, I hate you.* I was picking up my phone to put my earbuds in when I heard it. A smack. And silence. Mom's voice the undercurrent of a placid river, Garrett's door closing, her footsteps passing my door and out to the kitchen. I held my breath.

When I asked her about it, she laughed, pulling her head back, eyebrows raising at me. "How could you think that? He threw his controller against the wall. He is grounded until I decide otherwise." She shook her head. "You know how impossible he is."

I watched her, shuffling through contracts at the dining room table, artists whose shows she wanted for the gallery, and then I went back to my room. I knew the way a controller sounded when it hit things; Garrett threw his around all the time. But maybe I'd heard wrong. I hadn't really been listening.

"Arden?"

I startle at the voice, snapping back to the library, eyes lifting from the Cindy Sherman book. I was studying her composition before the memory bubbled up and took over.

Vanessa Flores is standing in front of me. I haven't talked to her since health class ended last year. We'd been part of the same group project. We'd made a *Jeopardy*-style game, but with the definitions of different genders and sexualities.

"Hey," I say. Her lipstick today is a matte pastel pink, a perfect complement to her golden-brown skin. She's wearing overalls and a Hawaiian shirt underneath. No one but her could pull off an outfit like that. Her dark curls are loose around her face.

She asks me about my summer. I answer. I'm still half in the memory, not quite in my body, and I feel like a hologram of myself.

"I love Cindy Sherman," she says, pointing at the book, open to a photograph.

"You know her?"

She widens her eyes. "Of course. Photography is my jam."

"Oh." I didn't know that. I open my mouth to ask her whether she uses film or digital, but the bell rings.

"See you later," she says with a smile, starting for the door.

"Bye," I say. I shut the book and watch her go.

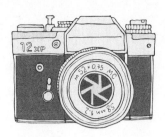

CHAPTER ELEVEN

"SHE LIVES!" DAD MOCK-GASPS WHEN I WALK INTO THE kitchen Saturday morning. He's sitting at the counter, reading the comics.

I roll my eyes, selecting Froot Loops and milk for my breakfast

"You've been holed up in your room all week, I wasn't sure," he says, raising his hands. "I was beginning to think I'd hallucinated my own daughter."

His voice is louder than usual, and he's smiling at me. Like he was the week after he talked to Mom. I look at him a little too long and he wiggles his eyebrows. "Do I have a booger hanging out of my nose? What's up?"

"Nothing." I sit down.

"Any more news from the gallery?" I'd told him last weekend, after I got home from hanging with Jamie, and he'd whooped so loudly it startled me into laughing.

"Nah, they sent me all the information after I emailed them my confirmation. I'm going to call into the lab for an enlarged print of my photo today. I'm supposed to go hang it next weekend." I grimace.

Dad props his chin on his fist. "And you're nervous about that."

"I don't know." I shrug. "I've never done a gallery installation before."

"You've seen your mom do one, though." He mentions her with an ease that doesn't feel quite real. Too casual. His eyes don't move from mine.

I look down at my cereal. "It's not the same."

"Want me to come?"

"Dad. I can do it."

He grins. "Of course you can." He folds the newspaper. "Any plans tonight?"

I shake my head.

"I have a paid opportunity for you, if you're willing." He gets up, refilling his mug from the coffeemaker. "I have a date with an old friend tonight. Can you watch your brother? I know he hasn't apologized to you yet. You don't have to talk to him, just be around the house and be your usual responsible self."

I raise my eyebrows, but it's not because he wants me to look out for Garrett. "You have a date?"

He laughs, waving his hand. "That's old-people speak for hanging out."

I guess that's true. Mom called her woman friends her girlfriends, no matter how many times Garrett snickered.

"His name is Will. A pal from my party days." He's referring to old Capitol Hill, the bars and community houses he used to hang in.

"Sure." I shrug. "How much?"

"Ten bucks and I order you pizza?"

"Done." And we shake on it.

Saturday passes slowly. Thanks to my Jamie-and-Caroline-avoidance strategy, I'm way ahead of the game on my history essay. It's not due until next Friday, the last day of school before winter break, and I need something to do during lunch. So today, I don't do much. A math assignment, a little bit of studying for French. After lunch, I put my earbuds in, letting Tegan and Sara blast into my eardrums, and open my photo cabinet. I want to find ones that are good. Ones I might want to submit. The thought of my work being out there for everyone to see, to judge, is scary. But knowing at least one photo was good enough to be chosen for a gallery tempers the fear, turns it into something I can mold, instead of something that shapes my every move.

Just most of my moves. But not all of them.

Dad sticks his head into my room around five. "Garrett should be back from soccer practice in about thirty minutes. Pizza should arrive around then, too. I'm taking off to meet my friend."

I give him a thumbs-up and he disappears. I take my earbuds out, listening through my phone speaker so I can hear the doorbell.

Thirty minutes later, the pizza arrives. I wait a couple minutes and then dig in. It's not like Garrett and I would eat together anyway.

After another thirty minutes, I've killed half the pizza and Garrett still isn't home. I look at my phone. He hasn't texted me. Of course. Does this mean I have to contact him? Probably. My pride growls in my chest, but I promised Dad.

Where are you? I ask.

Back in my room, I keep looking through photos, but I can't focus. Garrett usually gets a ride home from one of his friends, so there's no reason for him to be late. Soccer practice ends at five, and it doesn't take that long to get from the field in North Seattle back to Capitol Hill. I look up the travel time in Google Maps. There's a little traffic, but not enough for him to be this late.

Still no response text. I go to the front window and peek out at the curb. Dad left his car. I only have my permit, not my license, but still. Dad is finally out of the house, finally in a good mood. I don't want to ruin the night for him.

I find his car key on the hanger next to the front door and slip on my shoes. I'm not sure exactly what I'm going to do, but I have a half-formed idea: I can drive to the field. Maybe Garrett will be there. I grab my phone and my wallet and head out of the house.

Getting the car out of its spot takes me way longer than it probably should. I'm so nervous about hitting the BMW behind it that I inch back and forth until I finally pull out onto the street. I try not to imagine all the neighbors watching my ordeal.

On the road, I grip the steering wheel so hard my knuckles turn white. It's already dark out, and raining, and I'm not a very good driver. I stop too soon and press the gas too suddenly, and I almost run a STOP sign because I'm too busy scanning the crosswalk for pedestrians. I take the street route to the field, because there's no way I'm getting on the freeway.

As I approach the field, I can see the floodlights are on. Maybe they're still there. Except those lights never go off. That doesn't mean anything. I park, but I can already see the field is empty. I sit in the car, leg shaking up and down. Where is he?

Still no response to my text. I take a deep breath and call him.

No rings. It goes straight to voicemail.

I try to think. He usually goes home with a teammate. His closest friends on the team are Stefan and Victor. I could call their parents. Of course. I should have done that first.

But I don't have their numbers. Maybe in the league orientation packet?

I drive home, hoping the whole time that Garrett will already be there. Even though he'll probably try to get me in trouble for taking the car if he is. I will blackmail his ass if he even thinks for a minute he can get away with that.

When I get home, the parking spot is still somehow empty. It takes me almost ten minutes to get back into it. The whole car smells like anxiety sweat when I'm done, but I can't park it somewhere else, or Dad will know.

Garrett isn't back. Of course. I rifle through Dad's bedside table, his dresser, looking for anything with the league logo on it. Finally, in the kitchen junk drawer (because that makes sense?) I find what I'm looking for: the team roster, with parent contact information.

I dial Stefan's parents first.

"I'm sorry, we didn't give him a ride tonight," his mom says. "Let me know if I can help in some way."

Victor's dad says the same thing. "I think I saw him talking to the coach, though."

The coach's number is there, too, and I stare at it. This is getting out of control. How do I know these parents won't say something to Dad at the next game? And the coach definitely will. I can picture it: Oh hey, did Garrett get home okay the other night? Oh good, I wasn't sure, your daughter called asking about it.

And just like that. Busted.

It's not like I'm doing anything wrong. I don't even know why I'm doing this. I should just call Dad.

I pick up my phone and it rings, making me shriek and drop it. Shaking my head, I pick it back up.

Garrett's calling.

"Where the fuck are you?" I don't even bother to hide my anger. Let him yell at me again.

But he doesn't. "I decided to take the bus home. It's just taking a long time. Can you chill, please?" His voice sounds weird.

"Are you okay?" I ask.

"I'm fine. I'll be home soon, okay?"

"Okay."

We hang up, and I sit there, staring at the cold half pizza on the counter, adrenaline dissipating. Opening Google Maps, I check the transit time for buses from the field. It tells me exactly what I'm thinking, and I wait there for another half hour, until I hear the back door unlock.

Garrett shuffles in, dragging his soccer bag. I sit up straight. He shuts the door and jerks in surprise when he sees me.

"Jesus," he says. "What are you doing?" His voice still sounds weird, slower than usual.

"Waiting for you." I cross my arms. "You're almost two hours late."

"I told you." He rolls his eyes. "I took the bus." He walks past me, putting his hand out against the wall as he turns the corner. I follow him.

"It takes an hour by bus."

"My timing was off."

"Bullshit."

He stumbles over nothing and keeps going.

"You're drunk," I say to his back.

He stops. "No, I'm not."

"And now you're lying."

He turns, jaw clenched. "You sound like Mom."

The words sting. "What were you doing?"

He doesn't answer, just keeps walking toward his room.

"I drove all the way out to the field. I called Stefan and Victor's parents. I almost called Dad."

"Good for you!" he yells, whirling around—or at least he tries to. It turns into a stagger, and he barely catches himself on the wall. "You get to be the good one again! Like always!"

"I'm trying to take care of you!"

"I just wanted one fucking night out of this house!" he shouts. "One night where I don't have you or Dad on my back. It's like a depressing-ass morgue in here! Mom's gone. She's not coming back. She's moved on. She sucked anyway. I'm happy she's gone." He spits the last words at me, and I stare at him, mind blank, arms curling around my body. He turns and stomps the final few steps to his bedroom and slams the door behind him as hard as he can.

I stand there, tears blurring my eyes. I can't move. Everything is crumbling around me. I force my legs to walk, to take me into my own room, make my hands shut the door, and stumble to the bed, gasping for breath. I curl up, pull the covers over my head, squeeze my arms around my chest, and close my eyes. Inhale. Exhale. Inhale. Exhale.

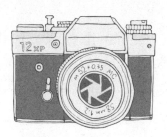

CHAPTER TWELVE

I WAKE UP HOT AND SUFFOCATING UNDER MY COMFORTER AND thrash it off me onto the floor. Silvery light is drifting through the blinds. I paw my bedside table but my phone isn't there. It's not in my bed either. The light tells me it must be morning, but without my phone, I don't know what time it is. My feet prickle when they hit the carpet, my zombie limbs coming back to life. I'm stiff all over, still in my jeans and hoodie from yesterday. Slept-in clothes feel gross, like they're imprinted on my skin. I change into sweats and a different t-shirt and shuffle out to the kitchen.

I see my phone first, on the counter where I must have left it after Garrett came home last night. And then I see Dad, emerging from the tiny half bathroom off the kitchen. He says a cheery hello and I mumble, sinking onto the stool and checking my phone. It's eight in the morning. Dear god.

"Want some breakfast?" He prods the eggs in the pan and I nod. Two seconds later there's a plate in front of me.

"You were out cold when I came home last night," he says, sitting across from me with his own plate. "So was Garrett. Everything go okay?"

"Yeah," I say out of habit, without thinking. Fuck. Eyes on your plate. Eat.

"He didn't give you a hard time?"

"He was late," I say.

"Oh?"

I stuff a big bite of egg into my mouth, waving at it, raising my eyebrows. Buying time.

"Morning," says a creaky voice behind us. Garrett stumbles up and looks at our plates. His brown hair sticks up at every angle, a pillow line creasing his face. Dad crosses back to the stove and serves up a plate for him.

"Heard you got home late last night," Dad says, light and easy, biting his own forkful of food.

"Uh," Garrett says, half-closed eyes opening slightly. "Yeah. I was."

"He decided to take the bus home for some reason," I say, rolling my eyes. Garrett glances at me. After a minute, he nods stiffly, jerking his shoulders up in a shrug.

Dad chuckles. "Whatever floats your boat, I guess." He eyes us both. "You're talking. Or at least, you're standing next to each other."

Garrett jerks his shoulders again. "Yeah. I was dumb. I'm sorry." He doesn't look at me, eyes fixed on some point on the far wall.

"It's okay," I say. I know that's the best I'm going to get from him. And he owes me now.

Dad smiles. "All right! That's good enough for me. Garrett, you're ungrounded. You wanna sit down?"

"Nah. I'll eat in my room."

"Okay."

When he's gone, I turn back to Dad. I don't know why I covered for Garrett, and the not-knowing is a thin veil, something I might tear in a moment with one wrong word. "How was your friend-date?" I put the last word in quotation marks with my fingers.

Dad smiles down at his plate. "Really excellent. We met up for happy hour at the Unicorn, talked for a few hours, and went to Lost Lake for some pancakes when we finally got hungry. I haven't seen Will in so long. We had a lot to catch up on."

He doesn't say anything more. I finish my food and slide out of the room, back to mine, and close the door.

Flopping onto the bed, I stare at the ceiling, last night running through my mind. The way Garrett's anger froze me in place. Jamie is right. I do shrink when people get mad. But it wasn't just that.

I'm happy she's gone, Garrett had said. I knew he and Mom fought a lot, but I didn't know it was that bad. Except maybe that one time, if I heard right. I always tried to avoid making her mad whenever I could. When she'd get upset I'd just nod and apologize and stay quiet, even if I hadn't done anything wrong.

He's happy she's gone.

Am I happy about it, too?

I stay curled in my bed watching Netflix most of the day, shaking my head when Dad peeks in to let me know he's going grocery shopping and to ask me if I want anything. When he leaves, I start *To All the Boys I've Loved Before* for the third time. It's my current favorite movie. There isn't any sex, and not even much kissing, but it's still romantic and fun. If I dated someone, I would want it to be like Lara Jean and Peter. Except, you know. With a girl.

A tap on my closed door makes me look up.

"Come in," I say.

The door opens. Garrett stands there, hands in the pockets of his blue joggers. I wait him out as he looks around my room, and finally he fixes his eyes on the rug near my bed.

"Thanks for saving my ass earlier."

I shrug.

"Why did you do that?" he asks.

"I don't know." I pause the movie, sitting up.

He side-eyes me, frowning.

"For real." I sigh. "What you said. Do you really mean that? About Mom?"

His turn to shrug. He runs a toe along the floor. I'm about to unpause the movie and ignore him out of my room when he speaks again. "Kind of. I don't know. Sometimes I really miss her." His voice cracks, and I watch him, my chest tightening. It's been a long time since Garrett showed any emotion that wasn't apathy or anger. "But most of the time I don't. Does that mean I'm a bad person?"

"No." The word is there before I can even think about it, and I know it's true. He finally looks at me, blinking fast, eyes glittering. I pick at the comforter. "I don't know if I miss her either. I don't know if I *don't* miss her. I just haven't thought about it. I try not to. Like, actively. Every time I do . . ." I shake my head. "I just don't get it."

He slides down the wall until he's sitting. "We talked about relationships in health class the other day."

"Are you dating someone? Is that who you were out with last night?"

He glares at me. "No! It was just me and a couple of other guys from the team. We hung out in the park across the street for a while and one of them had a forty." He's silent again. "We studied the Power and Control Wheel."

He's talking about health class again. I watch him, trying to follow his train of thought.

"It's about, you know." He opens his mouth, then closes it again. "Bad relationships. The cycles they go through."

The room feels smaller suddenly, like it's shrinking around us, and I get that feeling again, like I want to wrap my arms around my chest and hold tight.

He looks at me. "It was a lot like Mom and Dad's relationship."

"Dad isn't abusive," I say instantly.

"I know." He takes a deep breath, closing his eyes. "It's Mom. Mom is."

"No." I shake my head.

"Come on. They'd be fine for a while, until Mom found something to get mad about. It was always stupid shit, too. And she'd ice Dad out for a while, he'd be following her around like a puppy, and then they'd have one of their fights—"

The bedroom door closed behind them, the house drawn tight like a rubber band about to snap. I shake my head again. "Everyone fights."

He snorts, shaking his head. "Fine. Whatever." He scrambles up, vanishing out of my room. I surge to my feet, almost tripping on the end of the comforter, and slam the door shut behind him.

Yeah, Dad and Mom fought. A lot. Maybe their relationship wasn't healthy. But it wasn't abusive.

⁂

I want to talk to Jamie about what Garrett said, but on Monday he's with Caroline all day, and it's not something I can just text about. How the fuck are you supposed to talk about things like this? Hi Jamie, my brother thinks my mom was abusive. No way.

On Tuesday, I sit in the back of the library for lunch again. I've got my earbuds in; I'm listening to music, doodling on a piece of paper while I stare at the wall. Movement catches my eye, and I see him.

Jamie, at the entrance.

Shit. I forgot to give him an excuse today. I'm so used to going to the library now that I just headed straight here. I didn't even text.

He looks around and spots me, and it's too late.

I pull out my earbuds as he winds toward me through the tables. He stops when he reaches my table. I can see him taking in the sheet of paper, blank except for the random swirls and eyes and trees I've drawn all over it.

"Hey," he says slowly.

"Hi."

He looks at the paper and back at me. "You're not studying."

Fuck. I'm busted. "No."

"Why aren't you . . . why are you . . ." He gestures around the library. "What's going on? Are you . . . avoiding us?"

Us. So they're an *us* now, him and Caroline. Are her friends all part of that *us*, too? Are they all some group now, all of them friends without me?

"Yeah." My voice comes out tiny.

"Why?" His forehead is knit together, arms dangling limp at his sides.

"I . . ." My voice cracks. Oh no. I cannot cry, not here at

school. "I just . . . don't really feel comfortable with Caroline's friends."

"But . . . you haven't even talked to any of them! Except for Emma. But still. You haven't even given them a chance." His cheeks are red and splotchy now. This is frustrated Jamie, and an angry lump swells in my throat. Is he really this oblivious?

"Why do I have to?"

"What do you mean?"

"Why do I have to give them a chance?"

"Because! I'm dating Caroline! And you're my friend, and I don't want to choose between you, and if you would just get to know her—"

"I don't want to!" I yell. The librarian shushes from the front, glaring at us. I lower my voice. "I don't want to get to know her! Or her friends! I don't like her, Jamie."

"I can't believe this." Jamie's hands clench into fists. "So you've just been pretending this whole time to support me. To be excited for me."

"No, I—not at first, I tried, but—"

"Were you actually even studying in here?"

"Yeah." I sound defensive. Like I'm lying. But I did study. Not always, but most of the time.

"Wow." He stares at me. "I don't even know what to think."

Oh no. He looks seriously angry. "I'm really sorry." I don't know why I'm apologizing, but it feels like the only thing I can say to keep him from storming out. From leaving me forever.

"I don't know. I need . . . I think I need a break." He looks around, swallowing. "I just need to think."

"What does that mean?" I whisper.

"Not forever." His voice sounds half-strangled. "Just. Like. Can we not talk for a while? Just till I figure out how I feel about this."

I can't get any words out, so I just nod. He whirls and walks out as fast as he can, the back of his neck bright red. I stare down at the paper, tears pooling and spilling over, my face hot. I fucked up. Somehow. I'm not even sure what I did. But Jamie and I are on a break from our friendship now, and it's all my fault.

CHAPTER THIRTEEN

ON WEDNESDAY, JAMIE'S NOT IN SCHOOL. WE HAVEN'T TEXTED in days, not since before the fight. I know he and his moms are on a plane to Minnesota right now for their yearly Christmas visit with Lisa's family, who spoil Jamie like he's still two years old.

I go to the library, of course. My heart hurts like a black hole, but a tiny part of me is relieved that I don't have to make any more excuses for not sitting with Caroline's friends at lunch.

Garrett is back to not speaking to me unless he has to, and even then, he confines it to as few words as possible. I mostly try not to think about what he said, or my fight with Jamie. Instead, I distract myself with the other looming monster in my mind: the gallery opening.

The first day of winter break, I pick up the large-format print of my photo, rolled up and stored carefully inside a cardboard cylinder, and bus back up to Capitol Hill to the gallery. My stomach churns the whole way. I haven't set foot inside the gallery yet, or even walked by it; I have this weird fear that the second I do, someone who runs it will see me and decide I can't be in the show, that they made a mistake, that they didn't mean to include a high schooler's photograph in their exhibition.

The gallery looks small from the outside, just an old glass door with a hand-painted sign hanging on the inside: WELCOME TO THE RIOT. For the first time, I wonder if this is legit. It doesn't look anything like Mom's old gallery space in Pioneer Square, with its big windows and beautiful wooden doors leading into a huge space with vaulted ceilings. But I push the door open. A bell on the handle tinkles. A small, carpeted hallway stretches before me, and I follow it around a corner to another door, solid plywood, painted white. I try the handle and it opens, and I'm standing on the edge of the gallery.

The floor is pale hardwood from the door to an exposed brick wall at the far end, and the room is filled with white room dividers, some set up, some lying on the floor. It's a much bigger space than I thought it would be, and I realize it must be at the back of the businesses that sandwich it on either side. There are no windows, but the space is filled with bright light from the chandeliers overhead.

"Hi there!"

I jump, then notice the small booth to my left. There's a man standing inside it, smiling at me. He's tall and thin and white, with bleached hair faded along the sides to a long top. He's wearing a scoop-necked, flowy pink shirt. I realize I'm staring. "I like your shirt," I say. He looks so cool. I feel self-conscious suddenly, in my jeans and parka, a shapeless green raincoat on top.

"Thanks! I'm Ryan. He/him." He reaches out a hand and I shake it.

"I'm Arden. I have a photo in your show." I hold up the cardboard cylinder.

"Wonderful!" He leaves the booth, motioning me after him. "As you can see, we are setting up right now, so forgive the mess, but I'm so glad you're here. We've got a couple artists coming later, but you're our first of the day. Nat?" he calls out, and a short Black woman pops out from behind a divider.

"Natalia," she says, shaking my hand with a smile. "She/her." So this is the woman who sent the acceptance email. Her earrings are tiny porcelain oranges.

"This is Arden," Ryan says. "What are your pronouns, honey?"

"She/her," I say, a little dazed.

"Love it. She is here to give us her photo!" Ryan holds out a hand like he's presenting me to Natalia on a platter.

"Wonderful." Natalia's smile is as warm and bright as the color of her earrings. "Let's get started."

We lay the photo out on the floor, and she hums in appreciation. "This was one of my favorites," she says.

"Thanks." I smile.

"Have you had anything in an exhibition before?" she asks. I shake my head. "Okay. So the way it's done, we have all these dividers that we'll set up first. Once that's up, we take all the pieces and lay them out on the floor below the wall where we think they're going to go. That way, we get a visual read on what the exhibition might look like before we actually put it up, and we can move things around if we need to. So we won't put this up today." She looks at me, tapping her finger against her lips. "How did you want to hang it?"

I hadn't thought about that. "I'm not sure. A simple frame?"

She nods, looking down at the photo, then up at me again. "You're a high school student, right?"

I nod. Oh god. This is the moment. She's realizing they made a mistake.

"Typically, artists frame their own work, unless they plan to pin it, which isn't recommended. Most people don't want to put tiny holes in their art." She smiles.

I'm blushing now. "I'm sorry."

"Do not apologize," she says firmly. "You don't know something until you know it. I'm honored this is your first show. You should hit up the thrift stores, they always have cheap frames, and you can get mats at the art store across from the community college."

"Okay, cool." I nod. I wish I could sink into the floor. I should have looked up how to install a photo before I came here. She's being so nice to me, and it almost makes the embarrassment worse. I must seem like a kid who doesn't know anything.

"Once you've done that, come on back, and we'll take it off your hands." She smiles at me. "It was so great to meet you, Arden."

"Same to you." I manage a smile and another hand-shake, and she helps me roll up the photo and slip it back into the cylinder. A minute later, I'm out on the sidewalk. The embarrassment is whirling into shame. I can hear Mom's voice in my head: *Amateurish. You should have put more thought into this.*

Shut up, Mom. You're not here. I shake my head and set off for home. I'll drop my photo off and then I'll go find a frame.

░░░

If this were a normal winter break, Jamie would text me every day he's on vacation. I don't realize I'm waiting for the usual funny observations about his extended family and cute pictures of his aunt's new puppy (who must not be a puppy anymore) until they don't come. I keep checking my phone without thinking about it, and when there's nothing, no new alerts, I get this pit in my stomach. I try to give him space, but on Christmas Eve, I give in to the desperate pull inside me.

Besides, the gallery show is the Friday after Christmas. He'll be back by then, and I know he'll want to go.

I think.

Hey, I say. I was just wondering...do you want to talk soon? I know you said you wanted space and that's totally ok but I was just wondering for how long. And the gallery show is Friday and idk if you were planning to come but yeah.

I send it before I can overthink it and toss my phone onto the couch. On the coffee table, the tiny plastic tree glitters with tiny lights. We're not big on Christmas; Mom was an atheist. Is an atheist. She only abandoned us three months ago and already I'm forgetting to talk about her as if she's still here. So we usually put a few presents underneath the little tree, opened them Christmas morning with hot chocolate and pancakes, and called it a day. Both Mom and Dad moved far away from their extended families as soon as they were able, so there aren't any family celebrations like Jamie's that we have to go to.

And this year is even less festive. Dad only remembered to put up this tree three days ago.

A choking sensation rises in my throat and the tree blurs. I blink back the tears. It's stupid to cry over Jamie. It's not like he's my boyfriend or anything. He's just a friend.

My best friend.

The only friend I have.

Arden, if you don't learn how to socialize, you're going to end up alone, Mom used to say.

Or, *Jamie's not always going to be around to be your buffer.*

Or, *Are you sure you're not interested in him?*

No, Mom. No, I'm not.

I push off the couch and head for my room. Sometimes it feels like it's the only place her voice can't reach.

"Are you ready?" Dad calls through the bathroom door Friday evening.

I stare at myself in the mirror one last time. My hair is combed, my skinny black pants lint-rolled, and I'm wearing a pin-striped button-up I got from the men's section of the thrift store a few days ago. I like it. But something's missing.

"One more minute!" I riffle through the small bag in the bottom drawer below the sink. Straightening up, I look myself in the face and take a deep breath. I'm going to do this.

A little bit under each eye, smudged in, and at the corners of my eyelids. I remember exactly what the YouTube tutorial said to do, partly because I was obsessed with the YouTuber's hair. She'd dyed it lavender, but it wasn't just a flat pastel purple; there were all different colors woven in, like natural hair colors have.

There. I look a little more rock and roll now. More like how I want to look. It's only the second time I've worn eyeliner since my ill-advised freshman-year school photo. I take a deep breath and open the door.

Dad smiles. "You look great, honey. I'm getting Patti Smith vibes."

"Who's that?"

"What?!" He pops his jaw open in horror. "I've failed in my fatherly duties. This must be rectified."

"Sure." I laugh at him.

He grins, then tilts his head up like he's remembered something. "You got a special delivery."

I follow him to the kitchen, and there on the counter is a beautiful bouquet of flowers. Pink and yellow roses, interspersed with daisies. My heart starts to pound. Is it from Jamie? Why would he send flowers? I haven't heard from him in a week. He never answered my reminder text.

"Here." Dad hands me an envelope.

The handwriting on the outside is familiar. Too familiar. My ears start to ring a little bit as I pull out the card inside.

It's from Mom.

A little bird told me you have your first gallery showing today! Remember me when you become a famous photographer.

Love, Mom

I stare at the words. They hardly make sense.

"How did she . . ."

"I told her, honey. I thought she'd want to know."

"You told her?" I look at him. He's grinning, but it starts to slip, and I remember what I need to do. I smile. It feels like a death mask. "Thanks, Dad."

His face lights up with relief. "I know you kids haven't talked to her yet, but she asked about you both the other day and I thought I should pass the good news along."

"Yeah! Totally!"

"Well." He looks at the flowers, then back at me, still smiling. "Shall we?"

The street outside is cold, the sidewalk still wet from the afternoon rain, but the night sky above us is clear. He rambles on about Patti Smith as we walk, and I half-listen, thumbing my phone screen awake over and over. My body feels numb, his words coming from far away. Still no text from Jamie, and I texted him hours ago. A reminder. Just in case.

I wish we weren't taking space. I need to talk to him about this.

About Mom.

After three months, and this is her first contact? Flowers? And a card telling me not to forget her? I squeeze my free hand into a fist inside my jacket pocket.

Someone rounds the corner and I have to dodge aside, behind Dad. The surprise brings me back to my body as Dad chuckles. I fall back into step beside him.

"Where was I? Oh yeah. Just listen to *Horses*," he says. "Her seminal work. First album. One listen."

"Sure," I say, and he pumps his fist.

The hallway behind the gallery's glass door is lit by a blue-white bulb, and people flow in and out, some gathered outside smoking and laughing. I sneak glances as we pass: someone in a leather jacket covered in patches, a girl with her head tipped back and tattoos crawling up her neck, two boys kissing against the building's wall. In the hallway, we pass people whose genders I can only guess at, but won't, because I know that's rude and it doesn't matter anyway. Everyone seems to know each other, and everyone is older than me.

People fill the gallery, hands curved around wine

glasses. Dad heads to the open bar to get a beer and I hover by the table of food, eyeing the crackers and cheese. I don't want to eat though. Someone might see me eating and that would be weird. I'd be chewing, and what if I accidentally choke on a cracker crumb, or take too big a bite, or they try to talk to me while my mouth is full? A glass of ginger ale is safer. I pour one and sip it, even though I hate carbonated drinks.

I wander into the crowd, trying to find the open spaces so I don't accidentally brush against anyone. The photographs are merciless in their beauty, almost painful to look at. They're mostly portraits or action shots: of drag queens in stark black-and-white, waving from the top of a float; protesters defending themselves against police at a Black Lives Matter march; two people wrapped around each other in a bed, shot from above, in muted colors. There are a few landscapes: water bursting from a giant dam, an old house almost swallowed in vines. I wonder where my photo is.

I turn a corner, down one of the divider hallways, and there it is on the white wall in front of me. Seeing it is like a punch in the stomach. I look at it, look at him, at Jamie's face, his brows knitted slightly, eyes focused upward on the testosterone caught mid-draw into the needle. I remember standing in front of him while he sat on the bed, lifting the camera so the syringe filled the foreground and then turning the lens until the syringe fuzzed out and he sharpened into focus. The golden oil holding the testosterone complements his ginger hair, the freckles standing out on his nose, his skin almost translucently pale. The print is so big, so detailed, you can see his pores, but it's not ugly. It's just human.

My throat tightens. Pressure swells in my sternum, like crying and drowning at the same time. I want to leave but then I'll have to go talk to Dad, and if I talk to anyone I'll definitely cry, so I go to the bathroom and lock myself in a stall.

The walls are a sickly green. I stand in the stall and press my head against the door, but I don't cry. I take out my phone and there's a text on my screen. From Jamie.

I open it.

hey i'm really sorry but i can't come to the gallery opening tonight. caroline is mad at me and i have to go fix it, i'm really sorry, next one i promise

My heartbeat fills up my entire throat. I stare at the screen, the words separating from each other, separating from their meaning.

hey

sorry

can't

fix

promise

next one i promise

Next one. Because there are so many galleries lining up to show my photos. Okay, Jamie. I'll get right on that.

I shake my head. My brain feels fuzzy, like someone plugged it into an amp and turned the distortion way up. It's not Jamie's fault he's not here. Well, it is, because he did something to make Caroline mad. Maybe it was me she was mad about. Again. But that's not Jamie's fault.

But he waited until now. He waited, and left me hanging, wondering when we were going to talk, if he was going to come at all. And now this? Casual, as if there hasn't been silence between us for the last week.

Maybe Mom was right. I should have seen this coming. I should have made other friends.

A burst of chatter fills the bathroom. People. I wait until they're all in stalls and then I leave. The music is louder now out in the gallery, some thumping four-four beat, and the lights are dimmer. I wish I was at home, curled in my bed in front of a movie. I look back at my photo and there's a girl in front of it. Or at least, I see the back of her head, her dark curls hanging to the middle of her back, fanning out in a cloud above her black leather jacket. She's my height, medium-tall, and curvy. Her jeans are black, too, a studded belt around her waist and gold slip-on sneakers on her feet.

She turns, and I recognize her. It's Vanessa.

"Arden!" She smiles like she's been waiting to see me. "This is your photo."

"Yeah," I say, and my voice comes out weird. I clear my throat, but she doesn't seem to notice.

"It's so beautiful," she says. "I didn't know you were a photographer, too."

"I mean, I wouldn't call myself a photographer," I say. "I take pictures sometimes."

"You have a photo in an exhibition," she says. "I think that qualifies you as a photographer."

I shrug. Her smile wavers. "I guess," I say. Force a smile.

"We did that health project together last year, right?"

It's probably weird that I'm still standing in front of the bathrooms. So I walk over to her. "Yeah, with Feldman."

"Right!" She points at me.

"Are you in honors classes?" I ask. "I feel like I never see you."

"Yeah, for math," she says. "Writing isn't really my thing. And like. I don't really feel comfortable in honors classes."

I nod. I'm pretty sure I know what she's talking about. Most of the kids in the honors classes are white. I first noticed it last year, when I dropped out of honors chemistry and switched to regular chemistry instead, and I was one of two white students in the class. The teacher was extra nice to us, as if he was relieved we were there. After a while, I realized what was happening. The way he acted, how the classes were split up—that was the institutional racism Ms. Maldonado was always talking about.

"Arden?" Dad calls my name and I turn. He walks up, smiling at both of us. "Who's this?"

I introduce them and he shakes her hand, then puts an arm around my shoulder, gazing at the photo. "I know you showed me this before, but it's even better like this. Really good work, honey."

"Thanks." I stare at my toes. Every second in front of Jamie's face reminds me of his texts. His betrayal. Mom's words in my head. *You're going to end up alone.*

"How much longer you want to stay?" Dad asks.

"I could go," I say.

"You sure? We haven't been here that long."

"I've seen everything. I can come back anytime."

I can feel him looking at me. "Okay." He fumbles in his jacket pocket for his phone. "Hang on, let me take a photo of you and your picture."

"Dad." I glare at his chest.

"Come on! This is your first show. Gotta remember that."

"I can take a photo of both of you, if you want," Vanessa says.

Dad thanks her profusely, handing her his phone, and turns me to face her as she backs away. She gives a thumbs-up and asks us to smile. I manage an approximation.

When the photo is taken, he grabs it. "Stay there!" he says. "I want a photo of just you."

Finally, finally, just when I think I'm going to burst out sobbing in front of him and Vanessa and the impossibly cool people standing behind him, smiling at us, admiring my photo, he's done and we're leaving.

At home, I stand in front of the mirror, staring at myself. The eyeliner is dark—too dark. I look like a teenage raccoon. What a stupid idea. I take a baby wipe and scrub the eyeliner away until my lids are red.

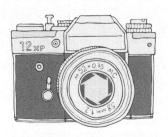

CHAPTER FOURTEEN

I DON'T TEXT JAMIE BACK. LET HIM WONDER IF I'M MAD AT HIM or not. Let him be the one on the other end waiting.

He texts me the next morning.

omg we have to meet up, i have to tell you something

I stare at the screen. I want to hurl my phone into the wall. But I don't. Okay, fine. If he wants to pretend what he did was okay, I will, too. We can meet. I'll act okay for a few minutes, and then I'll let him have it. I'll tell him exactly how he's hurt me.

Jamie wants to meet for brunch at Lost Lake, but I convince him to go to a coffee shop instead. A coffee shop is easier to leave quickly. I don't want to sit there waiting for my food, putting on a happy face.

I practice deep breathing all the way to the coffee shop, but the second I see his shock of ginger hair, my stomach turns over.

Jamie opens his arms for a hug and the gesture makes me stop on the sidewalk. We're a few feet apart, in front of the doorway. People dodge around us.

He lowers his arms. "What's wrong?"

"Are you serious?"

He takes a step back. "You're mad at me."

"Fucking duh! You ditched me last night! Again!"

"I told you why. I had to, Arden."

"This wasn't just a movie night," I said. "This was my first-ever exhibition. You were the one who got me to do it. And you flaked out for some girl." I twist my mouth around the words like they're bitter fruit.

"Caroline isn't some girl," Jamie says, enunciating every word. His face is flat and rigid, a look I've never seen. "She's my girlfriend."

"And that means she gets a magical free pass out of being a jerk?" My voice is loud. A couple passing us throws glances our way and then at each other. My face burns, but I'm past caring enough to stop. "She's a fucking liar."

"What. Are you. Talking about." He crosses his arms.

"Remember? Our 'little friendship'?" I put the words in air quotes. "She said it. I know she did. I was there. I didn't mishear her. She lied, Jamie."

"I don't believe you." His words hit me like a slap. I try to speak, but I can't. "You're jealous of her. You're jealous that you're not my only friend." I start to say no, I'm not, but he barrels onward. "I can't believe this. I came here because I wanted to tell you, even though you don't want to hear it—I know we were taking space, but you're still my best friend, and I wanted you to know—I wanted you to be the first to know that we had sex last night, but all you can think about is yourself."

I'm in a glass bowl, watching him, his words muffled. They had sex? Last night? When he should have been at the gallery?

"She told me this would happen." He shakes his head. "She was right. You don't get it."

"What." I force the words out. "What do you mean."

"You're aro-ace. We're not." He shrugs. "You can't understand what it's like, to fall in love, to want to be with someone like that."

"Fuck you."

Jamie's head jerks back.

"You've changed." I clench my fists. "She's changed you. She's not good for you, Jamie. She's a liar. I don't trust her."

"Well, I do." Jamie's eyes are brick walls. "If you don't get that . . ." He swallows. "We can't hang out."

The words hang in the air like our breath in the cold, not touching me. I'm numb. I stare at him and his face looks different. He's not someone I know anymore. He's not my best friend.

I turn and walk away, as fast as I can, and he doesn't call after me. Through Cal Anderson Park, past the basketball players and the families and the dogs with their owners. Tears streak down my cheeks and I don't bother wiping them away. I can't think, I can't feel, I can't stop. Someone passing me stops, says something like, are you okay or what's wrong, but I ignore them.

Where should I go? I can't go home. Dad is there, Garrett is there. I don't want them to see me like this. I don't know how to talk about this.

I let my feet carry me, up a few blocks, one street over from my house, and on toward Volunteer Park.

The stairs in the water tower are slick with moisture, my footsteps echoing on the metal. When I get to the top, I'm breathing hard, sweating from the walk and the climb. No one is there. I sit on a bench and stand up again, pacing around the top of the tower. This doesn't feel real. Everything feels far away. Everyone is far away. Everyone leaves me. First Mom. Now Jamie. People I thought cared about me. Loved me, even. I think it's possible to love your friends. Everyone treats that word like it's china, precious, only for special occasions, but that's never made sense to me. I love Jamie. And not in the way he loves Caroline. If he really loves her. If that's what he meant when he said I couldn't understand what it's like to fall in love. To want someone in that way. What way? Sexually? He says it so easily, as if one follows the other, as if you can't separate them.

If that's true, then he's right. I'll never understand. I'll be alone forever.

I curl my fingers around the iron bars on the tower windows. The Space Needle juts into the sky, and behind it the mountains, white and still across the flat blue of the Puget Sound. The iron is so cold it burns my fingers, and I shove them under my arms. I'll stay up here for as long as I can. It's quiet, and the mountains are beautiful. The mountains never change.

Breakfast, homework, Netflix, repeat. The rest of winter break slides by outside my bedroom window. I try not to think about Jamie, try to keep myself numb. This is the way things are now. I'll be alone, and it will be fine. I won't have to sit with Caroline and her stupid friends at lunch, I won't have to make up equally stupid excuses not to, I won't have to feel like shit every time Jamie flakes out on me. It's better this way.

The first morning back to school, I drag myself out into the kitchen. The flowers Mom sent are starting to wilt. I haven't thanked her for the card yet. I know I could just email her, but I don't even know where to start, and I don't want to talk to her. I glare at the flowers for a minute, and then grab them out of the vase, crushing them into the garbage. It feels good.

None of our cereals look appetizing. I stand in front of the fridge, but I can't make myself pick something. Finally, I just put on my shoes and leave without breakfast.

When I walk into second period, Jamie isn't there. I sit down in my usual spot. I don't know what else to do. I get the reading out and stare at it, the words splitting into letters without meaning.

"Dude, that's my seat." Tanner's voice makes me look up.

Jamie must have arrived when I wasn't looking, because he's sitting at the desk where Tanner usually sits, on the far side of the classroom where the teacher moved him after he wouldn't stop bothering me.

"There's no assigned seating. I can sit where I want." Jamie stretches out his legs, throwing an arm over the seat back.

Tanner's buddies jostle each other, snickering.

"Tanner." The teacher glares at him. "Find a seat."

Tanner looks around. His eyes fall on the open seat in front of me. Jamie's seat. He glances at me and smiles. "Fine." He saunters over.

My teeth clench. He smirks at me and slumps into the seat. I want to stab my pencil into the back of his neck.

"Are we going to be okay in that spot?" The teacher raises an eyebrow.

"Absolutely." He stretches his arms backward, into my space.

I lean back and glance at Jamie. He's texting under the desk. The tips of his ears are red, but he doesn't look my way.

If this is what he's willing to do for Caroline, then he's right. We're done.

CHAPTER FIFTEEN

THE NEXT WEEK, I'M SITTING IN THE LIBRARY WHEN VANESSA slides into the seat across from me. Her lipstick is a deep plum. "How are you?"

"I'm good." I close the book I'm reading. "What's up?"

"Not much." She taps her nails on the table. "Actually, I was looking for you."

I raise my eyebrows.

"I want to start a photography club. I have for a while, and after I saw your photo . . ." She smiles. "I was wondering if you'd be in it with me."

I look down at the cover of the book, tracing the raised letters of the title. "I'm not really a club person," I say finally, shrugging.

"It wouldn't be a huge time commitment," she says quickly. "Maybe one day a week, after school. I'm going to teach the basics to anyone who doesn't know and then we'll talk about what's next, what projects we want to do, whether we want to work as a group or individually." She watches me. "I just thought you might be into it when I saw your photo. It was so cinematic. I could see his focus, how much the testosterone means to him, but I could see you, too, your relationship with him, in the camera's gaze? It was beautiful."

I can tell I'm supposed to speak now, thank her, something, but nothing comes. I fold my arms, gripping my elbows. I'm wearing a giant sweater but I feel naked, like she reached right through the camera lens and ripped it away. I can hear Jamie's voice: *You'll have to let someone see eventually.*

"I only need five people to register an official club," Vanessa says. "Please?" Her chin juts forward slightly, head tilting, and I nod.

"Okay," I say, and she smiles, hands clasped together, thanking me, and then she's gone. Camera-flash gone. Did that really just happen?

Dad texts me on my way home, telling me he's meeting up again with his friend Will after work and won't be home until dinner. When I walk in the house, Garrett isn't there either. Select soccer season is over, and the school season hasn't started yet. So he's probably with his friends. Hopefully not drinking.

I toss the mail on the counter, microwave some pizza, and shut myself in my room. The pizza tastes like cardboard, but I wolf it anyway, trying to focus on the reading. I keep picking up my phone, but there's nothing there. The only person who ever texted me besides Dad was Jamie.

Finally, I slide the book across the carpet and lie down, staring at the ceiling. Earbuds in and I'm thumbing through Spotify, looking for something to listen to. All my favorites are boring. I want something new.

I check the Discover Weekly playlist and a name jumps out: Patti Smith. Dad's fave. Well, maybe not fave, but he did go on and on about her. I open the album and hit play on the first song.

The piano saunters in, and then her voice, a laconic growl, something about Jesus. The guitars whine out behind her voice as the drums kick in, picking up a little speed. I'm in the song, seeing it like a photograph, a series of snapshots. Someone leaning on a parking meter, and Patti watching that someone. A girl. Is Patti Smith gay?

I'm captured by her voice, winding around me. Her voice is like Hayley Kiyoko's gaze from the photograph above my desk: It takes charge. Patti knows what she wants, what she's singing about. Patti knows who she is. The guitars bubble and wail, the drums steamrolling faster and faster, a train out of control.

I see Vanessa's face, her dark hair like a cloud, lips a smiling purple. I wonder what she's doing right now. Her room is probably as cool as she is. I want to know which photographers she likes. Who she has on her walls.

I'm near the end of the album when I hear the back door slam shut. The footsteps are heavier than usual, but I know it's Garrett. I scramble up and open the door as he passes, and he glares at me.

"Mind your own business," he snaps, and disappears into his room, but not before I see him stumble a little bit. I want to say something, but I don't know what it would be, and he clearly doesn't want to talk to me. I stay, staring at the hallway, at a photo on the wall across from me. It's one of Mom's. I haven't really looked at it in so long, but now it seems weird that it's still up. It's a photo of me as a baby, at the Oregon Coast. I must have just learned to walk, because I'm toddling out way ahead of the camera lens, just one tiny kid on a vast shore stretching away to an ocean horizon jagged with rocks. Was she worried about me, or was she lost in the image, only thinking of the picture? Where was Dad?

I want to take it down, but I stand in place, unable to move. She's gone, but she's still here, like a shadow on my every move. Piano rings in my ears. The album is back at the beginning. I step back, cranking it up, and slam the door shut—slam it in her face.

⣿⣿

Friday is the first day of Photography Club. Not an optimal day for an after-school activity, but it was the only day the art teacher could stay behind. So Friday afternoon, I dodge swarms of students, fighting upstream to the back hallway. In my head, a mantra repeats: You can still leave, you can still leave, you can still leave.

The hallway is deserted when I get there, everyone already cleared out, ready for the weekend. I stop a few steps away from the classroom. I don't have to do this. I could go home, avoid Vanessa whenever I see her in the hallway.

And keep being alone. I think of Jamie, his arm around Caroline at her locker yesterday, lips locked together while I walked by. Me, the invisible girl.

My jaw clenches, and I take the last steps to the door.

The teacher looks up when I walk in. She's young, Asian, with black hair in a sharp bob, wearing a paint-stained black t-shirt and impossibly clean, dark blue jeans. She smiles.

"I'm Ms. Lim. You must be here for the club."

I nod. "I'm Arden."

"Hi, Arden. Make yourself at home." She sweeps an arm out to the empty classroom and I perch on a stool at the back, behind an easel. There's still a corkboard propped on it, a small drawing of a dick in the corner. Classic.

"Hi, Ms. Lim!" It's Vanessa. I watch her from around the easel, hair spilling over the shoulders of her long forest-green peacoat. She shrugs it off, piling it on a table, and riffles through her huge backpack. Binders, books, a sweater all scatter across the table as she hunts for something in the depths. Journey to the Center of the Earth: Backpack Edition.

She hums with satisfaction, pulling a camera bag out. It's small. A Canon manual point-and-shoot. She uses film, too.

I clear my throat. "Hey."

She doesn't hear me.

I stand up.

"Oh my god." She clutches her chest. "You scared the shit out of me."

"Sorry." I move carefully around the easel and slouch up to the other side of the table.

She looks at the clock, then smiles at me. "You beat me here. Did you bring a camera?"

I hold up a hand and slide back to the easel, lifting my backpack out from behind it. I unzip it, finding the bag nestled to one side of my books, and lift it out.

"Pentax K1000," I say, and her eyes light up.

"Can I see?" She sets her camera down, and I hand her mine. "Wow. I love old cameras." She turns it around, looking at the lens.

"My dad gave it to me when I was twelve," I say.

"He seemed nice at the gallery." She glances up at me. "Are you two close?"

"Yeah, I guess." I shrug, hoping she won't follow this line of questioning to its logical end. I don't want to talk about Mom. Don't want to see what pitying look will cross her face.

A knock sounds at the door and we both turn. Marc

leans against the doorway, head pushed forward slightly, like he's peeking in at us. "This the club?"

"Yes!" Vanessa lights up. Her teeth are so white.

Marc does a small fist-pump and joins us. He and Vanessa shake hands, introduce themselves, and then he smiles at me.

"Nice to see you, Arden. Didn't know you're a photographer."

"It's kind of my thing." I smile at him. Even though our last meeting was awkward, he smiles back like nothing ever happened. Like we're friends.

He's a senior, I remind myself. He's just being nice to you because you know Jamie. You're not his friend.

We pull out chairs at the next table over. Marc digs into his pack and produces his own camera, a super-nice Nikon DSLR. He and Vanessa spar for a few minutes over which is better, Canon or Nikon. The room is warm, the late-afternoon January sun blazing through the windows. I look over at Ms. Lim, typing away at her laptop. It feels safe in here. Like I could actually show Marc and Vanessa my photos.

A couple other students filter in: two freshmen, their names evaporating from my mind instantly, who nod and smile and don't talk as Vanessa and Marc discuss agendas and possibilities for the club. We're a small group, but that's okay.

"Well, this is cozy," a voice drawls from behind me, and my spine stiffens. I know that voice.

"Hey, Tanner," Vanessa says.

He jerks up his chin in a nod, and then his eyes land on me and the smile closes into a smirk. "Hey, Arden."

I stare at him. I'm not wasting my breath.

"What are you here for, dude?" Marc tilts back in his chair, one hand gripping the edge of the table, considering Tanner with calm brown eyes.

"The club." He holds up his phone, gaze taking in the cameras on the table. "If all you fancy photographers allow phones."

"I'm using my phone." One of the freshmen, a girl with an acne-scarred face, lifts hers from the table.

Tanner crosses to us. I've never been gladder that the seats on either side of me are taken. But then he takes the one right across from me. Great. Now I have to look at his face for the next hour.

He turns the chair around and sits with the back of it in front of him, arms propped on top. "What are we talking about?"

"Possible photography projects, skillsharing, whether

we should have an agenda every week . . ." Vanessa ticks them off on her fingers.

"We definitely need an agenda," Marc says. "I've been part of too many clubs without one. People just end up goofing off."

"Skillsharing sounds cool," the other freshman says from behind a curtain of long bangs. His voice cracks on the second word. Tanner snickers.

Vanessa side-eyes him, but he's on his phone, texting someone. "Maybe a code of conduct, too."

Marc and I nod at the same time. He catches my eye and winks. I raise an eyebrow back. The bubble of safety is popped, my chest tightening. Tanner being here was not part of the plan. And why is he here, anyway? I can't picture him behind the camera. I can't picture him doing anything creative at all. He's only ever been a force of chaos, and I doubt he's suddenly changed. Most people don't. No matter how much you wish they would.

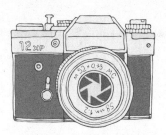

CHAPTER SIXTEEN

"ARDEN!"

The voice is perky and high-pitched, and I know it. Turning, I see Emma winding through the crowd toward me. The hallway is chaos, lockers slamming, people shouting, everyone getting ready for fifth period. I spent today's lunch in the library; the librarian knows me now and smiles whenever she sees me come in.

"Where have you been?" Emma asks when she reaches me. "I haven't seen you in forever."

"Oh." It's been almost three weeks since the quarter started. Three weeks without Jamie. I thought I was past having to make excuses, and I'm not ready for her question.

"I heard you and Jamie . . ." She trails off, mouth pulling down in a grimace.

So he told them all. Tears well up and I turn away from her, but I've already closed the locker. There's no sanctuary there.

"Oh god, I'm sorry. I shouldn't have said anything."

I shake my head and wipe my eyes. "It's fine."

"Are you okay?" Her round face is all concern.

No one has asked me how I am. There's no one who would, since I haven't told Dad about my fight with Jamie. I'm too tired to lie, so I just shrug. She glances down the hall.

"We should probably go to class," I say.

"I'll walk with you," she says.

The hallway is clearing out, and it turns out we're going in the same direction, out to the math portables. Once we step outside, the cold air is like a slap to the face. I zip my parka up to my chin.

"Caroline . . ." Emma hesitates. "She said you were . . ."

"Jealous?" I stare straight ahead. "I'm not."

"Were you and Jamie—"

"No."

"I'm sorry. We don't have to talk about it."

"Yeah," I say. "I don't really want to." Who knows where Emma actually stands? She seems nice, but she might just report everything I say back to Caroline.

Emma is quiet. Ahead of us, a few students disappear up the steps into a portable, the door swinging closed behind them. The courtyard is silent. She stops at the ramp to a classroom.

"This is mine," she says.

"Okay." We stand there for a second. I'm not looking at her, even though I can feel her looking at me. When I do meet her eyes, they're almost too kind. "See you later?"

She smiles. "Yeah. Have a good one."

"You, too." I walk away, toward my class. After a long pause, her footsteps creak up the ramp and the door squeaks open and closed again.

When I walk into Photography Club that Friday, Marc and the freshmen are already there. Music is blasting from an iPhone on a table; I recognize Janelle Monae's new song instantly.

"Arden Grey!" Marc smiles at me.

I grin. "I love this song."

"Right? She's serving some serious Prince vibes."

The freshmen wave at me. I still can't remember their names, but asking now would be too awkward. I wave back.

"Sorry I'm late!" Vanessa comes in, Tanner trailing behind her. I busy myself with my camera, popping in a new roll of film.

We circle around a table and quickly decide that we're going to take pictures on campus. Meet back in half an hour. Digital photographers will share if they want; film photographers will bring a photo next meetup. I'm hoping to tag along with Vanessa, but Tanner gloms on to her as soon as we break.

I head down the hall in the opposite direction, and Marc falls in beside me.

"Mind if I follow you?" He holds up his DSLR.

"Go for it."

The school is quiet, our footsteps echoing on the linoleum. A crumpled banner trails down a wall, and I pause, eyeing it. I could get a good angle, the hallway in the background, but is it worth spending the film? Marc kneels and rattles off a couple shots, tilting his camera to show me. The orange banner pops against the blurred background, the hall disappearing into darkness, the crumpled paper obscuring the banner's purpose.

"Mood," he says with a smirk.

I laugh. "Same."

We wander on. In my periphery I can see his head turn toward me a few times. Finally, I look at him. "What's up?"

"Heard about you and Jamie."

I had no idea Jamie talked to Marc outside of basketball. Does the whole school know?

"He was pretty upset."

My jaw clenches. "Yeah, well. So am I."

Marc stops and snaps another picture: an open, empty locker. He gazes at it, then at me. "Can I take a picture of you?"

I raise my eyebrows.

"Is that weird?"

I shrug. Then nod. "A little."

He smiles. "So honest."

"You asked!"

"You're right. Is it no-I-don't-want-to weird, or it's-awkward-but-I'll-give-it-a-shot weird?"

I grin. "It's awkward, but I'll give it a shot."

"Sweet." He points me in front of the bank of lockers, the open one to my left. I face him, turn side to side, striking fake model poses. He laughs, shaking his head. "Nah, just look at the camera."

I stand, looking into the lens.

"What did you and Jamie fight about?"

I watch the shutter close and open. "Didn't he tell you?"

"Yeah, but I want to hear it in your words."

I look away, down the empty hall. All the lights are out, the hall lit by the gray afternoon sunlight. "Caroline is a manipulative liar. She mocked my friendship with him to my face and then told him she didn't. And he believed her. Her, not me. I've been his best friend since freshman year." My voice cracks. "It's like, as soon as he met someone he could make out with, she was more important."

Marc lowers his camera. "I know what you mean."

I look at him.

"I always see that happen to people. They get with someone and they forget all about their friends." He shrugs, fiddling with the dials. "I don't know. I just don't get it. Maybe I haven't met someone who does that for me yet, but I can't see the person I date ever being more important than my friendships. Important in a different way, sure. But not more valuable."

"Exactly." I throw my hands out. The moment from the party pops into my mind: how he said he wasn't anything, and just as quickly ran off to find a drink. I want to ask him. I want to know. If he's like me.

He shakes his head. "I don't know. Caroline seems nice, but . . . why would you lie about something she said?"

"You believe me?"

"Of course." His dark brown eyes meet mine, and all of a sudden the tears are spilling over. I pull the sleeves of my sweatshirt over my hands, covering my face with the soft fabric.

"Hey. Oh man. I'm sorry."

I shake my head. I'm not mad at him. But I can't stop crying.

"Shit." His hand touches my shoulder. "Can I hug you?"

I nod. One arm wraps around me and I cry into his chest. I barely know him, but I feel safe with him. His arm squeezes, then loosens, resting on my shoulders, but he doesn't step back. Finally, I move away, and he does, too. The color of the linoleum clashes with his red basketball shoes.

"I think Caroline is bad for Jamie," I whisper, and the words leaving my mouth feel like a curse I'm bringing to life.

"Yeah." Marc's voice is low.

I wipe my face, staring over his shoulder, back at the crumpled banner, then up at him. "Sorry."

"What are you apologizing for?"

I shrug. "You don't even know me and I'm crying on you."

The corner of his mouth quirks up. "I know you a little bit."

"You're the captain of the basketball team."

"What is this, *The Breakfast Club*? I can't be friends with the nerdy junior?"

I laugh. "Oh, so I'm nerdy?"

He arches an eyebrow.

"Yeah, okay. I'm a nerd."

"That's not a bad thing," he says. "I'm a nerd, too. Just wait until we start talking about anime." He glances at his phone. "We should probably head back."

I bat the locker door closed with a satisfying bang, and we stroll down the hallway, turning back toward the art hallway. Marc wanders ahead of me, eyeing the hall for good shots. I pause, letting him walk farther, until he's right in the light from one of the windows.

"Marc!" I call out. He turns, and I take my shot.

"You got me," he says, pointing, and I take another. He grins, arms dropping to his sides. Click.

When we get back, Marc shares his banner shot, but not the ones he took of me, and I'm secretly glad. I don't know what I look like and I don't want Tanner to see. At the end of club, Vanessa lingers, talking to Ms. Lim about something. Tanner dips out, glancing back at her once before he exits. As I head for the door, she breaks away, following me.

"Do you catch the bus?" she asks, rummaging in her backpack until she finds what she's looking for: gum.

I nod and take a piece when she offers it. The gum is spearmint, cool and tingly in my mouth. She asks me which one, and I tell her. It's the same bus she takes. It turns out she lives in Beacon Hill, farther south and west of Capitol Hill, where she transfers from the bus we share onto another one.

"You're so lucky you live in the gayborhood," she says as we stand at the bus stop.

I laugh and scuff my toe along the sidewalk.

"I'm serious! I mean, I know a lot has changed, but . . ." She shrugs. "Legends never die, you know?"

We board the bus, finding open seats near the back. I tell her about my dad, the bars he used to hang out in before all the straight people moved in. How one night, he met a famous drag queen, and they stayed up all night on a coke bender.

"Oh my god." Her mouth opens.

"He made me promise never to tell Mom that he told me," I say.

"Your dad sounds fun," she says.

"What about your parents?"

She smiles. "They're adorable. They're both shorter than me and they're super in love. They kiss all the time. It's a little gross sometimes, but I don't mind."

I nod, but I'm thinking of Mom and Dad. I can't remember ever seeing them kiss in front of me and Garrett.

"We should hang out," Vanessa says.

"Yeah," I say. She's so close to me, our shoulders are touching.

She fumbles with her phone, and I tell her my number. A minute later, a text lights up my screen: a message from her, just emojis—a camera, a lipstick, a pink flower. For her last name, I'm guessing. She reaches upward to pull the cord for her stop, twisting into me, and for a moment her face is inches from mine. The signal for a stop dings and then she's up on her feet, smiling, swinging her backpack over her shoulder.

"See you Monday?"

I nod, and then she's out the door and into the darkness. The bus rattles away and someone else sinks into the spot beside me. But when I close my eyes, I pretend it's her.

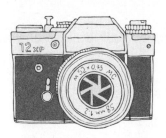

CHAPTER SEVENTEEN

I SET UP CAMP AT THE DINING ROOM TABLE ON SUNDAY AFTER-
noon to work on homework. Dad is sprawled out on the
couch, reading a book. I put some music in my earbuds
and crank it up, losing myself in my reading for class.

Voices make me look up. Garrett is standing at the
coffee table, saying something to Dad, and I take out
an earbud.

"—can't find it anywhere," Garrett finishes.

"What?" I ask.

"The book we're reading in English." He doesn't look
at me, riffling through the small stack of paperbacks on
the end table before crossing into the kitchen. I watch him
going through the pile of papers and books on the desk by
the back door.

I glance back at the screen. So close to done. Two
more pages.

"What the fuck?" Garrett's voice rings out from the kitchen.

"Garrett," Dad calls out.

Garrett doesn't correct himself. He appears in the doorway, a packet of papers clutched in his hand, staring at Dad. "What is this?" He holds it up.

Dad lowers the book, and his face goes expressionless. He sits up like it hurts every joint in his body.

Garrett flips through the packet. "Petition for divorce?"

Divorce. My whole body goes still, like I'm filled with lead. I can't move, only stare at him.

"She filled it out," Garrett says, and the words reach me as if from far away, like an aftershock. "She sent this to you?"

Dad nods. "I was going to tell you both."

"Yeah, well, you didn't," Garrett says. He's still in the doorway, like he's frozen, too.

"I'm sorry," Dad says, and his voice cracks. At the sound, Garrett moves, throwing the papers to the ground and running to his room. I stare at the empty space where he was, the kitchen like the out-of-focus background of a photo.

"Arden?" Dad's voice shatters the air encasing me.

I look down at my laptop, watch myself close it with

a click, gather my things, and slide toward my room. Dad calls my name again, but I can barely hear him, the pressure building in my ears. Divorce. They're getting a divorce. I know they said they were taking time apart. But this is something else. I can't be here right now.

I drop my things on my bed, pull on a sweater and coat, and then I'm down the hallway, past Dad who's gathering the papers, who says my name as I open the door, but I'm already gone, the sidewalk under my feet like a conveyer belt. I walk and walk and walk until I'm in Volunteer Park, but I don't go up the tower. I cross the park, out the other side, and into the cemetery, the gravestones silent watchers in the wet grass.

I pull out my phone and stare at the screen. No text messages. I want more than anything to call Jamie, and the knowledge that I can't pierces my lungs like a knife. I gasp, pressing my hand to my chest. This isn't a heart attack, but the pain in my sternum feels just as real. Tears streak my face and I don't wipe them away. I churn up the slope toward the back of the cemetery, away from the road winding through.

I don't understand why Garrett is upset. He said he was happy Mom left us. That she sucked. They fought all the time. I tried to stay out of it. He was always so rude to her. If he had just done what she asked, it would have been fine. *Would* it have been fine? I never talked back to her, and that didn't stop her from criticizing me.

I was just trying to be good. But it was never enough. I tried to be Jamie's friend, and it wasn't enough.

At the top of the hill, a huge black pillar beckons, and I lean against it, breathing hard. I'm crying in a graveyard. I am a living cliché.

My phone rings, and my heart leaps for a moment, but it's Dad. I sigh, accepting the call.

"Sweetie, where are you?"

In a graveyard, Dad. I can't say that. I tell him I'm at the park.

"Will you come home, please? I know this is hard, but we need to talk to each other."

I say I will and hang up. It feels dumb to go back as soon as I've left, but all the energy to run away is draining out of me, leaving me heavy and sad. The stone of the pillar is cold against my back. I push off, trudging back down toward the gate.

I don't know how to talk about this with Dad and Garrett. It's been four months, and we haven't spoken a word about it. Suddenly, that seems absurd.

The windows of our house glow golden as I approach, the lights on inside, night still coming too early. I swing open the gate and stand there for a minute, looking at the red brick and green lawn, the bare rose bushes under the front window, Dad sitting on the couch with his back to the street. Garrett crosses into the frame, bringing in a chair from the dining room table, and sits in it, staring down at his hands clutched in his lap. I want to take a picture, pause this moment before everything changes for good, but I didn't bring my camera, and my phone can't do this justice. I have to go in.

When I open the door, they both look at me. I bring over my own chair and wait beside Garrett for Dad to speak.

He sits forward, elbows on his knees, hands clasped together. "I should have told you earlier, and I'm sorry."

I expect Garrett to serve some smart-ass retort, but he's silent, eyes fixed on the carpet.

"Your mother sent me those papers a few weeks ago. We've been talking on and off for a few months, trying to work out our differences, but we couldn't. She wouldn't."

I raise my eyebrows. This is the first time I've ever heard Dad say anything critical of Mom.

He closes his eyes, taking a deep breath, and lets it out, looking first in my eyes, then at Garrett. "I wanted to protect you kids, so I didn't tell you anything. But I've been going to a counselor this past month, and he helped me realize that by not saying anything, I've also silenced myself, and kept you two from your own healing. I loved your mom. I tried to be a good husband to her, I did everything I could, but what I've realized is that it was never enough. And I know she was hard on you kids. Probably in ways I don't even know about, because I was so focused on making her happy." His voice turns to gravel and breaks, and I can't look at him. It's all I can do to stay in the chair. His sadness is a wave rushing at the dams I've built, and they're cracking. I'm cracking. "I'm going to sign those papers," he says. "I'm going to send them back to her next week. And I'm going to set both of you up with appointments to see my counselor. I want us to talk about this. We have to."

The silence grows in the room until I can't stand it anymore.

"I heard you talking to her. I knew you were talking to her. You were in your room and you asked her, 'What about the kids?'" The words are rushing out of me and I can't stop them, can't hold them in. "I just didn't know how to talk to you about it. She left us, but you did, too." I'm crying now, voice garbled through the tears. "You never asked us how we were doing and now you're all happy and hanging out with your friends and things are good for you, but she's still gone and it's not fair." I know I'm not making sense, but he's nodding like I am, and the nodding just makes me cry harder. There's so much more I want to say, but I don't know how to say it, so I curl up, wrapping my arms around my knees, and sob.

"I hear you, honey," he says. Beside me, Garrett shifts. "Please stay," Dad says.

"Why should I?" Garrett says. "You never stopped her." His voice is loud, and in my peripheral vision I see his hands curl around the edges of the seat, clenching hard.

Dad is silent. I look up at both of them. Dad leans forward, focused on Garrett, eyebrows drawn together in concern. Garrett is rigid in his seat, jaw tight, staring him in the eyes.

"You're right. You don't know what she was like," Garrett says. "Neither of you." He glares at me. "You were always the good kid. Perfect Arden and her camera."

I look down at my lap.

"Garrett," Dad says softly.

"No!" Garrett jumps out of his seat. "Don't fucking 'Garrett' me! You can't just say we're all gonna go to the counselor like it's gonna magically make everything better. I hate you. All of you. I'm done with this."

He whirls and stomps out. Dad doesn't say anything, just lets him go.

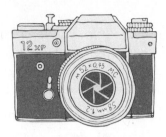

CHAPTER EIGHTEEN

I'M STANDING AT MY LOCKER MONDAY MORNING, TRYING TO summon up the motivation to shut it, let alone go to class, when someone taps my shoulder.

Vanessa is there with a gold-lipped smile when I turn. "I found you."

"I didn't know I was hiding," I say, and she laughs. It's too early and I'm too sad to be this witty, but I'll take it.

"What are you doing at lunch today?" she asks.

"Exploring the inner reaches of the library."

She laughs again. Have I always been this funny?

"I was wondering if you wanted to hang out. I usually eat with the other QA kids, but most of them are on a field trip." She pauses. "Wow, that came out way weirder than it sounded in my head. I promise I'm asking because I want to hang out, not because you're second best to my usual friends."

I'm already smiling. "No worries. Yeah. That would be cool."

We meet in the art room, where she's spread out her food in front of her: apple slices and peanut butter, a BLT, a water bottle. It's all in colorful Tupperware.

"Your lunch looks straight out of Pinterest," I say, sitting down across from her.

She rolls her eyes with a smile. "It's my mom. She still insists on making my lunches."

"Wow, that's so nice."

"It is. It would be even nicer if she would remember that I'm vegetarian." She plucks the bacon out of her sandwich and offers it to me. I crumble it onto my pasta. She sounds annoyed, but the kind of annoyed that people feel when they love someone so much, even their faults are endearing. I never felt that way about my mom. Her faults were something I had to forgive, and I didn't have a choice.

I push those thoughts away. "So you're in the Queer Alliance," I say, trying to sound casual.

She mumbles affirmation through a mouthful of sandwich. "Joined last year," she says. "When I came out."

"How did your parents take it?"

She shrugged. "They didn't really get it at first. Mom was like, 'But if you like boys, too, why does it matter if you like girls?' Even though I said I like people of all genders, not just boys and girls. But I think they've accepted it. They might not understand it, but they love me."

I eat my pasta, thinking about what she said. *People of all genders*. I know I don't like boys. I mean, as friends they're fine, and I can see how people find them aesthetically pleasing. But I've never crushed on a boy the way I've crushed on girls. Well, celebrity girls. Am I attracted to nonbinary people, too?

I notice she's watching me, chin in her hand, frowning slightly. I tilt my head.

"Are you okay with that?" she asks.

I laugh before I can stop myself. Her frown deepens. "Yes. Absolutely," I say. "Definitely." I'm babbling. "I mean. I do, too. I like girls, anyway. And maybe nonbinary people, too, I don't know."

Her face relaxes into that smile, like the sun peeking over the horizon until its light catches my face, and I'm warm under its glow.

"So what are you doing this weekend?" I ask, because I'm feeling bold.

"Hanging out with you," she says, and my heart starts pounding as fast as my current favorite Tegan and Sara song. We make plans, and then the bell rings.

On the bus home, I slip my earbuds in and turn on that song. Tegan (or Sara, I can't tell their voices apart) sings about a crush. And wanting to get a little bit closer to that person. Physically, even.

I don't know. I don't know if I want to kiss Vanessa or hold her hand. I don't know if this is what a crush feels like or if I just really want to be her friend. But I want to be close to her, and it's a different kind of wanting than when I first befriended Jamie. I don't know how to describe the difference, I just know that it exists. So I stop trying to figure it out, and I turn the song up and smile all the way home.

Dad and I are quiet and awkward with each other all week, and Garrett avoids both of us. He stays out later and later every evening, giving Dad the barest explanation when he walks in, and Dad doesn't push him. I know Garrett is supposed to see the counselor for the first time this Saturday, and I'm supposed to go next week, but I don't really see the point. If my family can't even talk to each other, how are we supposed to talk to a stranger? He can't possibly understand what we've been through. Sometimes I feel like I don't understand it, either.

Mom wasn't the worst. She was there. She bought me new rolls of film every time I ran out, and watched Audrey Hepburn movies with me, and took me to her gallery openings when I was a kid. She wouldn't have done that if she didn't love me. She didn't scream at us, or call us names, or beat us. Except. Maybe that time with Garrett, when I thought I misheard. What if I didn't mishear?

What if that wasn't the only time?

Thursday night, a loud crash from the living room wakes me up. Heart racing, I grab my phone. It's one in the morning.

Dad's door opens across the hall, and I'm sliding out of bed to pull on sweatpants because no way do I want to be pantsless if we're getting burgled, when his voice stops me.

"Garrett, where the hell have you been?"

I freeze in the middle of my room, then tiptoe to my door and listen.

"I was out," Garrett says, but his voice is too loud, and slurring. He's drunk again.

"This has to stop," Dad says, quieter now.

"Why?" Garrett is practically yelling.

"G, please." Feet moving, then a light thump.

"You can't block me from my own room!" Garrett says.

"Are you hungry?" Dad asks.

Silence.

"Just come in the kitchen with me. We had pizza tonight for dinner. We missed you."

"You didn't miss me," Garrett says, but his voice is lower now, more of a mutter.

"Well, I guess I can't speak for Arden, but I missed you," Dad says. "Come on. We got your favorite."

Garrett mutters something I can't hear. Footsteps, then a crunch. "Shit."

"We can clean that up in the morning," Dad says. "Come on."

I hear them move away, and then they must be in the kitchen, because I can't hear them anymore, just the occasional distant murmur. For a second, I think about sneaking out to listen. But overhearing Dad talking to Mom didn't make me feel any better that one time, and it feels wrong to eavesdrop now. This is just between Garrett and Dad.

I go back to bed and lie down, my heart slowing. If I'm being honest, I don't know if I've missed Garrett, exactly, but it's been weird without him—weird to watch him slip further and further away. He used to be so sweet, before he and Mom started fighting.

I think again of what he told me. What he thought about Mom. Maybe I should have listened.

<hr>

Photography Club is quiet that Friday. Marc, Vanessa, and I sit around talking for ten minutes past the usual start time, but no one else shows up.

"What do you wanna do today?" Vanessa asks.

Marc glances at me. "I'd be down to leave the school."

"That sounds good," I say. I look at the door, then up at the clock. If we leave soon, there's less chance that Tanner will walk in late and join us.

"Sure," Vanessa says. "Where to?" She wiggles her shoulders back and forth, smiling.

"What about the UW campus?" Marc says. "There's hella cool old buildings there."

"And the fancy library!" I jump up, and Vanessa laughs.

"The what now?" she asks.

"Well, it's really called the Graduate Reading Room or something, but it looks straight out of a British castle," I say. "You've never been there?"

She shakes her head. "I usually just hang out in my neighborhood when I'm not at school."

"You'll love it," I say, and we grin at each other.

The bus drops us off across from the Burke Museum, or at least, what used to be the museum. The whole parking lot is under construction so they can expand the building. We walk up along the north edge of campus.

Vanessa gapes at the huge houses across the street.

"That's Greek Row. Where the frats are," Marc says, and Vanessa makes a face.

We turn right, down the main road into the center of campus. The grass is bright green and wet from the rain misting down from the gray sky. It's so light, I don't bother to put my hood up, but Marc shivers, pulling on a bright yellow beanie.

We point and shoot whenever we feel like it, wandering off the road and down the paths through the buildings of the university. I snap Marc sliding down the railing of one building, and Vanessa leaning in the doorway of another. I attempt to climb one of the cherry trees on the quad and end up koala-clinging to the trunk halfway up while Vanessa snaps a picture and Marc laughs. I stick out my tongue and he rattles off a burst of pictures. As we all laugh, I can't help thinking how much Jamie would love this. How well he'd get along with Vanessa; I already know he likes Marc. I can just see him goofing off with the three of us, all of us laughing together.

My heart hurts, and I push the thoughts away.

We walk out onto Red Square. "That's where the Reading Room is," I say, pointing to Suzzallo Library. We slow down, pausing to scan the carved statues standing on buttresses across the brick and sandstone facade, the huge stained glass windows above the massive doors. One wide stair step at a time takes us into the library, where a stone staircase splits off from the lobby in either direction. We head for the left staircase, spiraling up to the second floor.

Vanessa's jaw drops as we step through the doorway and into the Reading Room. Above us hang two rows of chandeliers made of dark iron and amber glass, stretching away to our left and right. In both directions underneath the chandeliers are two rows of long wooden tables, each one with small reading lamps set into a divider running the length of the table. Students sit throughout the room, reading or working on homework.

We cross the first row into the center aisle and turn slowly, taking it in. Even though I've been here before, I still feel small and hushed, in awe of the vaulted ceiling above us, the walls lined with shelves full of old books. Silvery light drifts in through the tall windows, the same ones we saw from the outside.

"You weren't kidding about the castle vibes," Vanessa whispers. She lifts her camera, pointing it down the center of the aisle, and snaps a picture. A student nearby looks up at the click of the shutter and, frowning, returns to their paper.

We exchange raised eyebrows and stifled giggles and move toward the south end of the room. Marc drifts away toward the bookshelves, trailing his fingers over the spines; Vanessa strides ahead of me to the display at the end of the aisle. I slow down and stand looking up at the windows, following the shafts of light down into the library. I raise my camera and find one cutting down between two chandeliers. When I trip the shutter, calm settles over me. Even though everything is fucked-up, I still have this.

We stay in the room for a while, circling quietly, until we end up all together at the doorway again. Marc tilts his head toward the exit, shrugging, and we follow him out.

"I want to read in there, like, every day," Vanessa says once we're outside again.

I smile.

Marc shoves his hands into his pockets, staring down at the red brick under our feet. He seems like he's somewhere else now, and I can't tell what he's thinking.

"We should get some food," I say, because I don't want the day to end.

Vanessa agrees, and Marc follows both of us.

University Way, otherwise known as the Ave, is just one block west of campus. It's lined with hole-in-the-wall restaurants, coffee shops, clothing boutiques, and a few bookstores, and it's teeming with students. Of course. It's Friday evening.

We end up walking north, several blocks up the street, farther away from the crowds, to a vegan Thai place. We order and wait, Vanessa and I chattering away. Marc is still quiet, chin on his hand, staring out the window.

"You okay?" I ask him finally.

"What?" He blinks, looking over at us. "Oh. Yeah. I just miss my parents. We ate out here a few days ago before they left on another trip."

"Are they gone a lot?"

"Yeah. Every few weeks. My dad's a professor, and he gets asked to come talk at a lot of different places. Mom's a financial consultant. She can work anywhere, so she just goes with him." He looks up, smiling at the waitress as she sets down our food.

We dig in. "What about you two?" he asks.

Vanessa describes her parents, her two older sisters who are both in college now, one of them engaged.

"My dad's a teacher," I say when it's my turn. "I have one little brother." I pause, stirring my tom kha soup. My heart is pounding. I've never said anything about my mom to anyone other than Jamie. Marc and Vanessa are quiet, like they know something big is coming. "My parents are getting divorced, I guess. My mom left us in September and my brother found the papers this weekend." What I'm saying is way too personal. I hardly know either of them. My skin crawls and I want to hunch my head into my shoulders, hide like a turtle.

"Wow." Vanessa's voice is soft and warm. "That sounds really hard, Arden."

I shrug, staring down at the golden soup, the vegetables bobbing in it like islands. "Sorry. I don't wanna be a downer."

"You're not." She puts out a hand and touches mine.

"You're good." Marc squeezes my shoulder. "We got

you." He grabs his plate of food with one hand, lifting it up. "Side note, though: this might be the best pad Thai I've ever eaten."

"Let me get some," Vanessa says, reaching for it with her fork.

"Wow, so you're just gonna jack my food like that?" Marc laughs, but I can tell he's teasing.

"Yes. Yes I am." Vanessa sticks a forkful in her mouth. "Oh wow," she mumbles around the noodles.

"So your mom . . ." Marc looks at me. "You miss her?"

I shrug. "I don't know. She wasn't . . . She was kind of . . ." It's hard to actually say it out loud, the word ringing in my ears. It feels like admitting something. Vanessa and Marc just wait. "Controlling," I finish. My heart is pounding.

"That sucks," Marc says. "I'd have a hard time missing her, too, if it was me."

"Thanks." Just hearing him say that out loud feels like he's lifted a weight out of my hands. They both smile at me across the table, and there isn't pity in their eyes, just witnessing. It feels good.

I don't know what Dad and Garrett talked about the night he came home drunk, but Garrett goes to counseling with only a little sulking on Saturday morning. Right after they leave, Vanessa shows up for our hangout.

"Wanna go thrifting?" she says when I ask what she wants to do. We're in my room after a brief tour of the house. She sits in the desk chair, spinning slowly, while I sit on the bed.

"Sure," I say. "Where at?"

She names one spot on Broadway, and twenty minutes later we're there, wandering the aisles. "So I've noticed you do a lot of macro photography," I say as we're flipping through the shirts. "What do you like about it?"

"Well, I like finding things other people might miss. Those little secret parts of everyday life. And I like that you can use close-ups to make something normal seem mysterious, or look like something else entirely. Like, when you can't even tell what it is?" she says.

"Wow, that's . . ." I pause.

"Weird? Boring?" She lets out a short laugh.

I was kind of thinking that, but I'm not about to tell her. Photos have always been a way for me to capture what's there, and I've never really understood the appeal of the kind of work Vanessa does.

"No, I've just never thought of it that way," I say instead, and that's true, too.

She side-eyes me. "You don't have to save my feelings."

"I'm not!"

She arches an eyebrow.

"Okay, yeah, it's not something I've ever been interested in." I remember what Marc said. "But it's just new to me, that's all, and if you like it, who cares?"

She grins. "I knew I liked you."

I can feel myself blush, and I move away, into the other room where the jackets are. She follows me, and we're quiet for a little bit, cruising the selection. I pull out a burgundy blazer, admiring it.

"You have to get that," she says from the other side of the rack.

"I don't know." I put it back.

"Arden. Try it on." She's got one hand on her hip now.

I pull it back out and shrug into it, hold out my arms, strike a pose. Vanessa claps. I walk over to a nearby mirror and look at myself. The jacket fits me perfectly. Dad would probably say it has a rock-and-roll vibe, too. Definitely something Patti Smith would wear. Not something I'd wear. It's not that I don't want to. But it's so far off from my usual t-shirt–and–jeans combo, my classic Seattle parka-and-raincoat situation. I don't know when I would ever wear it. That was Mom's litmus test for everything: practicality. Whether things made sense. If they didn't, it was a no-go. She questioned me whenever I did anything out of the norm, or what she thought the norm should be. And sometimes questioned things I thought were already the norm. *Why are you wearing that? Why are you going there? Why do you hang out with Jamie?* I stopped wearing anything that might catch her attention, stopped doing things she hadn't already approved of.

The only thing I didn't stop doing was hanging out with Jamie.

Tears blur my eyes and I blink them back furiously, but it's too late.

"What's wrong?" Vanessa asks from behind me. In the mirror, her round face is full of concern, and I avoid her eyes, pulling off the jacket and putting it back onto the hanger.

"Nothing."

"Yeah, okay. That's definitely not true."

I stand there, holding the jacket. "I just. I want this. It's just not what I normally wear."

"So? Branch out!" She throws her arms out, and it's so cute, I'd smile if I could.

"It's not that easy."

She tugs the jacket from my hands and turns, marching toward the register. I chase after her, asking her what she's doing, but she goes right up to the cashier and hands it to him, ignoring me as he rings it up.

"She'll pay for it," she says, jerking a thumb at me.

"You're the worst," I say, pulling out my wallet.

She just smiles.

At home, after we say goodbye, after we hug, after I notice that she smells like roses, I hang the jacket on my door and look at it, grinning to myself. It's mine, and this time Mom isn't here to question me.

The back door opens and shuts, and I poke my head out. Pots clank in the kitchen, and Garrett appears, heading for his room.

"How was counseling?" I ask.

He shrugs, passing me, and I start to close my door, but then he stops and looks at the wall next to me.

"It was okay," he says. Meets my eyes, just for a second. And then he's gone.

I look at the picture across the hall again, little me on the beach, the sand stretching away. Now I see it—how brave I was, walking out there alone. Maybe that was what Mom wanted to capture.

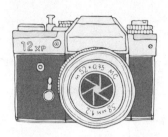

CHAPTER NINETEEN

THAT WEEK, I DON'T SIT IN THE LIBRARY AT LUNCH. I'M WITH the Queer Alliance now in the art room, at Vanessa's invitation. They only have official meetings every Wednesday, but they hang out most days of the week, or at least a few of them do. People flow in and out, some days more people than others, but I'm there every day. It feels good. Vanessa and I text most nights now, about homework, family, photography. She's not Jamie, but that's okay. She's Vanessa.

Thursday afternoon, I duck out of lunch for a minute to hit the bathroom. I do my thing, wash my hands, and stride out.

Right into Jamie, coming out of the boys' bathroom.

He jumps back right before we collide, and we're staring at each other before I can think to drop my eyes and avoid him like I have been for almost a month. His face is splotchy, his eyes red, like he's been crying.

Neither of us says anything. Neither of us moves. It's like we're playing chicken, each of us waiting for the other to break the spell.

"Are you okay?" I ask.

"I'm fine," he says. But his voice is watery.

I frown.

"I'm fine," he repeats, and sidesteps around me, heading for the stairs. I watch him go. I want to call him back, but the words are stuck in my throat. I should be mad at him. He picked Caroline. He threw me back into Tanner's jaws. Which, admittedly, hasn't amounted to much. Tanner's mostly left me alone. Sometimes he leans back in his chair and stretches into my space and sits sideways with his elbow on my desk, legs in the aisles, staring up front like he's totally innocent, but that's about it. Since the incident in bio at the beginning of the year, when Mr. Bones served him a detention and threatened his Jefferson High sports career, he hasn't been doing anything that might draw too much attention to him.

Jamie is gone. I turn and walk back to the art room, but in my mind, I can still see his tearstained face.

The next afternoon at Photo Club, it's just me, Vanessa, and one of the freshmen. Tanner hasn't been at club since a few weeks ago, and Marc is gone for one of the last basketball games of the season. I try not to think about how that means he's hanging out with Jamie. I wonder if Jamie has talked to Marc about why he was crying.

I come back to reality just as Vanessa suggests we meet back at the classroom in fifteen minutes. I nod along with the freshman, pretending like I was paying attention, and grab my camera.

Today, I feel like being alone, so I go the opposite direction from Vanessa, out toward the gym. I know I won't see Jamie. It's an away game. But my stomach flutters all the same. The first time he ditched me for Caroline, I learned about it there, from Marc.

But the gym is in use. I can hear a few ragged cheers as I approach. It's not full by any means. When I peek in the door, I can see why. Two guys are tangled together on the mat, in skintight singlets, one trying to hold down the other.

It's a wrestling match. So that's why Tanner isn't at Photo Club.

I spot him across the gym, sitting in the row of metal folding chairs on the Jefferson High side of the mats. He's in shadow, his gaze fixed on the two wrestlers held in the spotlight. It's a perfect photograph, so after a moment, I lift the camera to my eye, adjust the light meter, and trip the shutter.

When I lower the camera, he's looking right at me. I whirl and walk away, back down the hall, heart pounding. I must seem like a total freak. Like I have a crush on him or something. Why did I take that picture?

Because it was a good shot. I know it is. And I know Annie Leibovitz never let awkwardness get in the way of a good photograph.

Back at the classroom, we share photos and talk for a while. Ms. Lim trusts us to lock up now, and she's long gone. Eventually, the freshman says a quiet goodbye, bangs still covering his eyes, and disappears. It's just me and Vanessa, joking and smiling at each other.

"Hey, creeper."

Tanner's voice startles us both. He's there in the doorway, arms crossed. "I saw you take that photo, Arden."

"Good job," I say. Out of the corner of my eye I can see Vanessa watching us.

"So now that Jamie has a real girlfriend, you gotta find someone else to obsess over, huh?"

"Shut up."

He laughs, and the sound echoes down the empty hallway behind him. "Everyone knows you were in love with him. Too bad you got dumped for someone he could actually fuck."

I stand up. "Leave me alone, Tanner." His eyebrows raise for a split second. We face each other, and I can hear cars outside honking in the parking lot. People leaving the wrestling match. "What is your problem with me?"

"You just took a stalker photo of me," he says. "I knew you weren't asexual. That's not a real thing. You just want to be special."

"Are you serious?" Vanessa steps up beside me. "Seems like you're the one who's obsessed."

Tanner holds up his hands. "I'm just fucking with her. Not my fault she can't take a joke."

"Then you have a terrible sense of humor," Vanessa says.

"I took that photo because it was a good image," I say, turning every word to steel. "Believe it or not, not everything is about you. And you say I want to be special? You're the one who makes juvenile jokes with his friends and harasses me for no reason. You're an insecure piece of shit."

He stares at me and starts to sputter something out, but I interrupt him. "If you talk to me again, I'm reporting you to the school counselor for harassment," I say. "And I'll get Mr. Bones in on it, too." The school counselor doesn't mess around when it comes to harassment. She's scatterbrained, but she got a football player kicked out of school last year for groping a cheerleader's ass.

"And I'll back her up," Vanessa says.

"Fuck you both," he says, but it doesn't have its usual punch, and it's such a ridiculous response I laugh out loud. He steps back.

"Whatever, Tanner."

He seems like he's about to say something else, and Vanessa waves at him. "Either you go bye-bye or your sports career does, asshole."

He turns, and then he's gone.

My whole body is shaking and I collapse into my seat. I want to cry and scream and laugh at the same time. The adrenaline rushes through me like a drug, like the top of my head is gone and my body is filling up with oxygen. I close my eyes and sit there as his footsteps recede into silence. Vanessa pulls up a chair beside me and grabs my hand. I'm so full of nervous energy I can hardly feel it, but it registers somewhere. She's touching me. Her skin is on mine.

"Are you okay?" she asks.

I open my eyes and stare at the door. "I've never done anything like that before."

"He's such an asshole," she says. "So glad I dodged that bullet."

I look at her. "What do you mean?"

"We have a couple classes together and he kept trying to talk to me," she says. "I didn't really know him, and it was a little weird but then he showed up at club, and a couple weeks ago he asked me out. I said no, because um . . . no. So he stopped coming to Photo Club. I think the only reason he did was because he wanted to date me."

"Gross."

"I know, right?"

And it must be the adrenaline, but then I say, "So, do you like anyone?"

She smiles and looks down at our hands. "I do."

"Who?"

She shrugs. "That's my secret." She looks up at me, still smiling. "For now."

CHAPTER TWENTY

SATURDAY MORNING FINDS ME AT A SMALL BUNGALOW IN North Seattle that's been turned into a private therapy practice. Garrett and I are trading off appointments; he goes one week, and I go the next. The house is green with white trim and wide wooden steps up to a large front porch. Inside, across the pale golden hardwood floor, in what probably used to be the living room, a receptionist sits at a desk. She smiles when Dad and I come in.

"Hal! So nice to see you. Is this your other kiddo?"

I'm sixteen, not a kiddo, I want to say, but I just smile. "That's me."

"Great." She beams at me and hands over a small packet. "Just fill this out and we'll have you in with Dr. Benjamin in a moment."

We sit on the couch and fill out the paperwork, and then there are footsteps on the floor and I look up. A tall

Black man wearing brown wingtip shoes, dark blue jeans, and a sweater smiles at us. "You must be Arden." His eyes crinkle at the corners, and he nods at Dad.

I stand up and shake his hand.

"Come on back," he says, and I follow him.

The walls in his office are painted a pale yellow, and with the hardwood of the floor, the whole room feels warm. Or maybe that's just the heat from the wall heater. He's got a comfy armchair against one wall and a big rectangular window opposite the door that looks out onto the backyard. Across from the armchair, against the other wall, is a pink velvet couch with a coffee table and a small blue armchair beside it. I sit on the middle seat of the couch, right on the edge, looking at the bookcase beside the door. There are copies of the *DSM*-V and other therapist books, plus a whole row of books about social issues: racism, transphobia, poverty—it's all there. His bookcase looks like a college class—one I want to take.

The bottom row is fiction, some of the authors they make us read in English, some I recognize as classics, a few I've seen Dad read.

"Why do you have books here?" I ask.

"Sometimes I read between clients," he says. "It makes the room feel cozy, and it helps tell people a little more about me."

I can understand that. I wonder what my room says about me.

"So, what's on your mind?" he asks. He sits back in the armchair, one ankle propped on his other knee, hands folded loosely in his lap. I thought he'd have a notebook, and I say as much.

"It's all up here." He smiles, tapping his forehead.

I shrug. "You've been seeing my dad."

"I'm here for you," he says, but it's not the "here" he emphasizes. It's the "you."

My eyes sting with tears and I scoot back onto the couch cushion, staring at the grain of the coffee table. "I don't know, hmm, let's see: My mom left us, my best friend abandoned me, my brother is sneaking out to get drunk with his friends, and it turns out my parents are officially getting a divorce. Where do you want to start?"

"What's bothering you the most right now?"

Jamie's face, red and tearstained, pops into my mind. I stare out the window. "I saw my friend the other day. The best friend I just mentioned." I tell him the saga of Jamie and Caroline. He makes small listening noises now and then, but I keep my eyes fastened on the pine trees outside. "I don't know. Maybe I'm reading too much into this. But I saw him at school the other day and he looked really upset. I don't know. I shouldn't even care."

"Why not?" Dr. Benjamin's face is open and gentle, his eyes alert.

I lift my shoulders. "Because. We're not friends anymore. He said it himself."

"What do you want?"

I look down at my hands, clasping them together, rubbing one thumb over the other. I don't know how to answer the question, because I haven't thought about it. Jamie made his choice, and I let him.

"I can't make him be friends with me," I say.

"No."

"And . . . I don't know. I've been hanging out with some people. I mean, I miss him. But I can't carry everything. I can't be the one to fix things all the time. I've always been that person. I've always been the one to smile and nod and do whatever people want."

"Did you and Jamie fight a lot?"

I frown, glancing up at him. "No. We never did, before she came along."

"Where in your life do you smile and nod and go along with things?" There's no confrontation in his tone, just curiosity.

And I know exactly where.

"Mom," I say, and my voice comes out tiny, like a child's. He lets out a low hum, and I start crying.

━━━━━━━━━━━━━━━━━━━━━━━━━━━━━━━

Marc is back at Photography Club that Friday, full of stories of how our team pulverized the other one at last week's game. He doesn't say anything about Jamie, though. We don't split up for photos this week; instead, the film photographers are finally bringing in the ones they've shot over the past month. Which means Vanessa and I are in the hot seat. I let her go first. Showing the club my pictures isn't scary, exactly, but I'm okay with waiting a little longer.

She's got some funny ones of bathroom graffiti: the top of the toilet roll, so zoomed in you can see the pattern on the paper, and right above it—but blurry, because the toilet paper is the focus—someone's written *Shayla is a bitch* in bubble letters. There are extreme close-ups of three different letters written on the ancient chalkboard in Mr. Feldman's room: a *W*, an *H*, and a *Y*, the board visible through the chalk particles. "A triptych," she says, and we all snicker.

And then it's my turn. I spread them out on the table. First up is my shot of Tanner and the wrestlers, which turned out as good as I thought it would; they all admire it without any comments on the subject. Then I lay out my three of Marc.

"Speaking of a triptych," Vanessa says, lining the photos of Marc up beside each other. In the first he's just turning around, three-quarters to the camera, the light from the window catching his face. His eyebrows are raised in expectation. In the second he's grinning, pointing at the camera. And in the third he's looking to his left away from the window, the light falling on his neck, arms hanging at his sides, but he's still smiling.

"These are dope," he says now.

"Thanks." I smile down at the photos.

Later, on my way to the bus, he catches up to me. "Can I get copies of those?"

I say of course, and we exchange numbers.

"I should make you my personal photographer," he says.

I glance up the street. The bus is at the next block; if I don't go now, I'll miss it. "Thanks."

"Hey, what are you doing right now?" he asks.

"I was going to go home," I say.

He follows my glance this time, up to the bus. "That yours?"

I nod, but I don't move.

"You want to hang out?"

And I say yes.

In the daylight, with all the lights off and no people partying inside, his house is smaller than I remember. The door swings closed behind us with a heavy thump, our footsteps echoing in the entryway. He kicks off his shoes and drops his backpack, and I follow suit.

The house feels empty, and I tell him so.

"My parents are out of town again." He pulls a couple mugs out of an impossibly tall cabinet and turns on the kettle. "Tea?" He opens another cabinet and gestures to two full rows of different kinds, herbal and caffeinated. I pick a lemon hibiscus, and he grabs a jasmine green.

We carry the tea upstairs, carpet plush under my toes, past a couple closed doors until we get to another staircase. At the top, my jaw drops, and Marc laughs. "Welcome to my room," he says, throwing his arm out to the whole top floor.

There are windows on every side, and I can see out over the neighborhood to the west, the Cascade Mountains bright and cold in the east. He's got a queen-sized bed and a chest of drawers on one side, and against the other wall is a flat-screen with a couch in front of it, and multiple video game consoles.

"My brother would die for this room," I say, picking up the Xbox.

Marc flops down on the couch, smiling. I sit on the floor, at the small coffee table, and poke at the magazines he has. Mostly *Sports Illustrated*. I hold up the swimsuit edition with a raised eyebrow.

"I haven't looked at that yet," he says.

"Come on." I open it. A girl in the smallest bikini I've ever seen stares up at me. I know how I'm supposed to feel, and she's definitely beautiful, but that's all. Maybe I was wrong about Marc.

"You remember the party?" he asks.

"My first whole beer," I say, closing the magazine. "A truly momentous occasion."

"No way," he says. "I'm honored."

I roll my eyes and look at the shelf of DVDs. Every single one is some kind of anime show. He wasn't kidding about that. *Cowboy Bebop, Neon Genesis Evangelion*, all of Hayao Miyazaki's movies, and other titles I've never heard of.

"What about the party?" I ask, looking back at him.

He's on his back, staring at the ceiling. "You remember what I said?" He starts talking again before I can answer. "About how I'm not anything. I think I'm asexual." The words come out in a rush, and he's staring down the ceiling like it's an alien and his eyeballs are laser guns.

I look down at the magazine and put it carefully back in the stack, under the others. "I know."

"What?!" He turns over.

"Marc. Come on. I asked you about your orientation and you say you're not anything? And then you dip out?"

He covers his face with one arm. "You knew this whole time. Oh man."

"I mean, not for sure."

"It's just weird," he says. "My whole life I thought there was something wrong with me. And then Jamie mentioned asexuality one day and I was like, wait. I'm not the only one? And I looked up that word and it's just so perfect. It explains everything. I never think about sex.

Like, ever." He waves his hand at the stack of magazines. "I even tried, you know." He cups his hand and makes a jerking motion. "Nothing. I just have no interest in it. I want to date people, but how am I supposed to when everyone else wants to have sex? And expects me to want to?"

"I know."

"It's easier for you," he says. "People don't have stereotypes about girls and sex."

"Hello? Slut-shaming?" I turn my palms up.

"That's true." He takes his arm off his face. "But like, people expect guys to want sex all the time. They don't do that for girls."

"Doesn't mean it's easier. People still expect you to want to make out and have sex once you're dating someone, no matter who you are."

"You're right. It's just a lot of pressure. People think I want to bone anything that moves because I'm a guy, and doubly so because I'm captain of the basketball team. Don't even get me started on stereotypes about Black guys."

"Yeah," I say, and leave it at that, because he doesn't need me to tell him how fucked-up it is.

"I bet if anyone saw us leaving together, they'd probably think we're dating," he says, glancing at me.

"I mean, I like girls," I say.

He grins. "I know."

"What? How do you know?" I cross my arms.

"Same way you knew about me. I can see it every time you look at Vanessa. You are in loooove," he says, drawing out the last word.

"I am not."

He shrugs. "Suit yourself."

I trace the groove in the coffee table, the border along its edges, remembering Vanessa's fingers aligning my photos, how her dark eyes sparkled as she looked at them. We'd made plans for this weekend. A sleepover, at her house.

"That. Right there." I look up to see Marc pointing at me. "That smile. You like her!"

I cover my mouth, but he's right. I am smiling. "I don't even know what a crush is supposed to feel like," I say.

"Your face says otherwise."

I throw a magazine at him, and he throws a pillow at me, and then we're both laughing. He asks if I want to watch a show, and I say yes, and hanging out with him is so easy I don't notice the time go by until Dad texts me, asking if I'll be home for dinner.

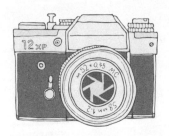

CHAPTER TWENTY-ONE

I WAKE UP THE NEXT MORNING WITH A TIGHTNESS IN MY CHEST, half excitement, half anxiety. The sun dapples its way across the ceiling, and I'm frozen in my blanket burrito, thinking about tonight.

Me.

At Vanessa's house.

For a sleepover.

I can't decide if I want to scream or throw up.

Dad was surprised when I told him last night where I was going this weekend and asked me if Vanessa was the same girl from the gallery. When I told him that I'd joined Photography Club with her, he raised his eyebrows, but not in a suspicious way. More like he was glad. If Mom had been here, I would have gotten the third degree.

If Mom had been here, I wouldn't have even made plans with Vanessa.

I start packing early. I have to choose the clothes I'm going to wear, and then, oh god—pajamas. Normally I wear a big shirt and underwear to sleep in, but that is not going to happen tonight. Finally, I land on my least-faded sleep shirt—one of Dad's old band shirts from the eighties—and a pair of bike shorts Mom got me when she wanted us all to be a cycling family.

Eventually I finish, and then I'm just waiting. I'm way too antsy to study, so I just flop down on my bed and mindlessly scroll through YouTube on my phone, looking for something interesting.

A notification pops up on my screen: an email. I glance at it, swipe it away, glance back to YouTube, and then I realize what I just saw.

This pressure fills my chest, like concrete weighing me down. I exit YouTube and pull up my email.

There it is.

Sender: *Evelyn Grey*

Subject line: *Reaching out*

I can't breathe. Months later, and here she is.

Mom. In my inbox.

I hover my finger over the subject line on the screen. Shut my eyes. Tap.

And open them.

Hi kids,

I know I haven't contacted you since I left, and I'm sorry if that was hurtful to you. I did send you flowers for your gallery show, Arden, but I haven't heard from you yet, so I don't know if they made it to you. Your dad tells me you two know about the divorce. I know this must be hard for you. I don't know if you've given it any thought, but I'd love for you to come live with me. I've got a wonderful little house here in San Francisco.

A few more lines about some gallery she's running and the new friends she's making.

Anyway, just thought I'd reach out and give you the option. Let me know.

Love,
Mom

I stare at the words until they lose all their meaning. "Reaching out." As if this is something we did to her; as if we've been ignoring her. And she made sure to tell me she sent me flowers. Good for you, Mom. You did the bare minimum, and you didn't even congratulate me.

White-hot rage floods my chest, and I realize my hand is clenched around my phone. I throw it onto the bed so hard it bounces away into the pillow. I push off my bed, walk to my door, then to the window, then out into the hallway. The house is empty; Garrett's at a game and Dad is out again. I don't know what to do, so I just stand in the living room, buzzing with energy and no place to put it. A million things flash through my mind: text Jamie, call Jamie, demand he talk to you, no you can't do that. I stomp into the kitchen and yank open the fridge, stare at it, slam the door so hard something inside rattles and falls, and then I scream.

I scream so loud the neighbors probably hear me, but I don't care. I scream and scream until my throat hurts and I start coughing. My mind feels like it's tied in knots. I stomp to my room and grab my phone again.

There's a text from Vanessa waiting for me. Something about how she's excited for tonight. I read it a couple times and it barely registers, but suddenly all the energy drains out of my body and I sit down on the carpet, still holding my phone.

It pings again. Why is everyone choosing this moment to text me? I want to look, but if it's Jamie . . . I don't know how that will feel.

But it's not. It's Marc, sending me an old Vine compilation.

I could tell Marc or Vanessa.

No. Not yet. I need to wait until I feel okay. I don't want them to see me like this. Whatever this is.

I toss away my phone, lie down on the carpet, and cry for a long time.

By evening, the anger and sadness have receded, and I just feel numb. I don't even feel anxious anymore. I hop the light rail to Beacon Hill, and when it arrives, I walk fifteen minutes from the station into the neighborhood. The houses here are a little more run-down than where I live, but still cozy, with chain-link fences enclosing lawns, some with toys scattered on the grass. Vanessa's house is white-shingled, two windows flanking the concrete steps up to a raspberry-pink door.

"I love this color," I say when she opens it.

"My mom picked it," she says, smiling, and I step inside.

"Is that her?" A short, plump woman appears. She crosses the floor in small, quick steps, grasping my hand.

"Arden. I'm Claudia. It's so good to meet you. Vanessa talks about you all the time."

"Mom." Vanessa mouths a *sorry* at me, but her mom leads me into the kitchen.

"Are you hungry? I'm making dinner right now."

"That sounds great," I say.

"Parmesan or cheddar?" She holds up two packages. I choose cheddar, and she grins. "A classic."

"Is Arden here?" A man pokes his head into the kitchen and grins when he spots me. He's got a trim, dark mustache to match his hair, grayed at the temples. "I'm Francisco. Nice to meet you." He crosses to the stove, embracing Claudia from behind. She leans back to kiss him and I look at Vanessa, who raises an eyebrow.

"I told you," she says.

"Told her what?" Francisco selects a knife and cutting board and begins chopping the onion Claudia hands him.

"About your shameless PDA," Vanessa says.

Claudia laughs like a church bell. "Shameless is right! No shame here." She winks at Francisco.

"Okay, bye!" Vanessa grabs my arm and I follow her out, her parents laughing behind us.

"They're adorable," I say when we're in her room.

She laughs, closing the door. I look around, taking in the pink carpet, the walls with their tiny arrangements of photographs in thin gold frames. On the wall beside the door, above an old wooden dresser, are two pictures: her parents, Vanessa with them, and a younger Vanessa, two teenage girls behind her, grinning on a sun-drenched beach.

"Those are my sisters," she says. "They're older. We visit my grandparents in Mexico every spring."

In a photo on the wall at the head of her bed, a pink flower blooms in darkness, the stem fading into the black background. It looks familiar.

"Percy Smith," she says. "He was one of the first macro photographers. It's from *The Birth of a Flower*. One of his most famous time-lapse photographs." She sits down on the bed, and I curl up in the red beanbag across from her. There's a table beside the bed, books and a laptop piled on top of it, and a laundry basket overflowing with clothes in the corner. Being here feels good. Safe. The anxiety is back, a little bit, but this time I think it's mostly excitement.

"So." She leans back, a small smile playing over her lips. They're bare today. "What do you want to do?"

We settle on a movie. Vanessa moves her bedside table out onto the carpet, setting her laptop on top, and lies on her stomach across the bed. I sit beside her, not too close. A few minutes in, her mom looks in on us.

"Door open," she says, leaving it ajar.

"Mom!" Vanessa hides her face with her hands.

"Well." Claudia shrugs. "We have to worry about girls now, too. Whose fault is that?" She winks at me, and a blush explodes across my cheeks.

"She is so embarrassing," Vanessa says when she's gone, dragging her fingers down her face.

I manage a laugh. "It's okay."

The silence is uncomfortable now, but the movie fills it, and I focus on the screen. The main actress has short hair, almost a pixie, with long, choppy bangs. I can't stop staring at it. My hair has always been shoulder-length, middle-parted, and it's longer now, spilling over my collarbone.

"I love her hair," I say midway through the movie.

"You'd look great with that cut," Vanessa says. She glances over. "I could cut your hair."

"What? No."

"My cousin is a hairstylist. She taught me a few tricks."

She sits up. "I promise I won't mess it up. If I do, we can go fix it."

I look at her, and then back at the screen. I have no idea what's going on, but the actress is in a shoot-out of some kind. "Okay," I say.

"Wait. For real?"

"Yeah." I slide off the bed. "Let's do it."

Francisco and Claudia are still in the kitchen, music blasting, and whatever this dinner is, it smells amazing. Their bathroom is small, a sink beside a toilet beside a narrow shower, and Vanessa drags a chair in from somewhere, plunking it in front of the sink. I sit down and watch her plucking things out of the cabinet behind me. She turns around with scissors, a comb, a razor, and a squirt bottle.

"Ready?"

I nod, even though I'm not so sure, and stick my head under the faucet at her direction.

The hair falls away in chunks at first. Vanessa is right; she's not a professional, but she does know what to do. It doesn't look terrible, and as the shape of my head emerges under her fingers, my face changes, too. It's not just a boring oval. There are angles, and cheekbones. She takes the razor and pulls forward the hair on the top of my head, turning it jagged with the edge of the blade, leaving a longer chunk at the side of my face. She blow-dries my hair, aiming the dryer from the back, putting some kind of pomade on her fingers and working it through.

When she's done, I stare.

"Do you like it?" she asks, biting her lower lip.

I look like a different person, someone with a much colder neck and the kind of hair I've always envied. Not short hair, specifically. But hair that says something about the person whose head it sits on. This hair definitely counts as rock and roll.

"I love it," I say.

I can feel her hand resting on my shoulder, and I want to reach up and grab it, but I don't. I just grin at her in the mirror.

Much later, when dinner is over, we lie on her bed talking. The door is open, but her parents are in their bedroom, with their own door closed. There's a sleeping bag on the floor, but I don't want to move to it yet. If I move, I'll break the spell, and the night will end.

"So, when did you know?" she asks.

I think for a minute. "I don't know," I say finally. "I was always into girl celebrities, not boys." I'm careful with my language. She doesn't need to know that my version of being into someone means holding hands, means wanting to be near them, but not in a naked way. Except maybe emotionally. Which is how I'm starting to feel right now—like my fear fell away with my hair and there's just me beside her on the bed, nothing holding me back.

"Saaaame," she says. "At first, I was like, do I want to be with them or just *be* them? Turns out it's both." We laugh. "I mean, boys are cute. I'd date one. But I'm more interested in girls right now." She holds my gaze with hers, and then her eyes shift, down to my mouth. My heart rate ratchets up. I know what that look means. I've seen it in countless movies.

If you don't learn how to socialize . . .

Are you sure you're not interested . . .

I'd love for you to come live with me.

Mom's voice blares in my head, her words flashing on the screen behind my eyes.

"I'll be right back," I say, and roll off the bed, not waiting for a response. I can feel my armpits sweating, and I shut the bathroom door behind me, leaning on the sink, staring at myself. I look different, but I'm not any different inside. I'm still the same girl who feels uncomfortable whenever there's a sex scene in a movie, who doesn't know what to do when someone's into her, who's too scared to even try. The girl in the mirror has cool hair, but she's still alone.

What if I kiss Vanessa, and I like it? What if I fall for her, and then she turns out like Caroline?

Mom left us after years of marriage and parenthood. How am I supposed to believe Vanessa really likes me? What if she kisses me, and I don't like it? What if she wants someone she can have sex with, and I don't want that?

Maybe Jamie and Mom were both right.

Vanessa smiles when I come back into the room.

"I'm super tired," I say. "Can we go to sleep?" I don't want to sleep, but I can't get back on the bed after the way Vanessa looked at me.

"Sure!" she says brightly, like nothing happened. We change into PJs silently, not looking at each other, and I slide down inside the sleeping bag, wishing I could disappear. She probably thinks I'm so awkward.

"Good night," she says, and the lights go out.

Dad's eyes go wide when I get in the car the next morning.

I touch the back of my neck. "What?"

"I feel like you had a lot more hair yesterday," he says with a smile.

I shrug, and he reaches out, squeezing my hand. "I love it."

"It's really different," I say. The confidence of last night is gone and now I'm wondering if I made a mistake. There's nothing to hide my face now. I'm out there, exposed.

"You'll get used to it. I think it looks fantastic."

I squeeze his hand back.

At home, I stare at myself in selfie mode, tilting my head back and forth. I've never taken a selfie, but I think I'm starting to understand the appeal. The more I look at my hair, the better I feel. It does look good.

I get up and put on my pin-striped shirt from the gallery opening, then I pull the burgundy blazer from my closet. Black jeans, bare feet, and eyeliner complete the look. Camera goes on the tripod, with the timer and flash attached, all the lights in the room off, and the curtains drawn. I climb onto my bed, sit on my knees, snarl at the camera. Click/flash. I set the timer again and bend sideways, reaching an arm toward the lens. Click/flash. I flip up the collar and purse my lips. Click/flash. I want them to look dramatic and overexposed, like a disposable camera but better quality. Like a Cindy Sherman photo, this new girl I'm wearing.

This new girl I could be, if I hadn't chickened out last night.

Now that it's morning, I'm confused. Last night, it just seemed safer to avoid the possibility of a kiss, avoid the conversation that might have to happen, avoid whatever Vanessa might or might not say. But in the daylight, I feel like I missed my chance.

My phone dings from the desk and I scramble off the bed to grab it, wondering if it's Vanessa. Everything was normal this morning, like we never had that moment.

It's not Vanessa.

Just one word.

Hey.

It's Jamie.

CHAPTER TWENTY-TWO

VALENTINE'S DAY REVIVES THE ROTTING CORPSE OF CANDY-
Grams and gives it a pink heart–covered background with choices of three different Hershey's Kisses for attachment. The cheerleaders are hawking hard on Thursday; their spring dance depends on it. I ignore the table like I ignored Jamie's text. He didn't send another. I want so badly to reply, but I'm too angry. He broke our friendship. A single text won't fix that.

"Good morning, historians!" Ms. Maldonado is wearing a black-and-white pantsuit with chunky gold jewelry today. History is bearable because of her; somehow her excitement makes it less like torture and more like mild discomfort. Today, we settle in for a documentary on the Black Panthers.

A knock at the door. Two cheerleaders poke their

heads in, one above the other like they're in a cheesy nineties movie. "CandyGram delivery!"

Ms. Maldonado sighs and motions them in, pausing the movie. They bounce down the aisles, dropping the paper cutouts. I stare out the window at the flat and leaden sky.

"Arden Grey!" I look up at the chipper voice and a Gram lands in front of me. My heart leaps. Jamie? I pick it up and read the message, as if the pre-printed words hold a clue.

Ms. Maldonado starts the movie again, but I just look at the Gram. If he sent it, what does that mean? What about Caroline?

At lunch I speedwalk to the CandyGram table and wait in line for five minutes, chewing one of my nails. Finally, I'm in front of a ponytailed cheerleader, her smile lip-gloss shiny, her eyes looking right through me. I hand her my dollar. The other cheerleader shuffles through the record of Gram purchases. My chest is tight, a river held back by a logjam, water pressing against my rib cage.

"Vanessa Flores."

"What?" I stare at her.

She lifts one perfectly drawn eyebrow. "Vanessa Flores? That's who bought you the Gram."

I stare down at the sheets in her hand. The cheerleaders glance at each other and I turn, losing myself in the crowd of people heading to fifth period.

I don't talk to Vanessa about the CandyGram, and she doesn't say anything about it during club time the next day. Over the weekend, we text funny videos back and forth, talk about what we're up to—she has a family thing, I'm just doing homework—and it starts to feel like the Gram is the elephant in the room. Our interactions rewind and replay in my head: Vanessa looking at my photo in Riot Gallery. Finding me in the library after school and asking me to help her start the club. The look she gave me in her bed last weekend.

Was that the only reason she talked to me? Because she thought I was cute and wanted to date me? I know logically that's a perfectly fine reason to talk to someone, but when I imagine our friendship in this light, my heart feels heavy and unmoored at the same time. Heavy with new truth, drifting on a strange sea with no map, no stars, no means of navigation.

But she's Vanessa. She wears a different shade of lipstick every day and takes macro photos of toilet paper and loves Tegan and Sara like I do. She's funny and honest. Just seeing her makes me smile.

Marc was right. I do have a crush on her. The way I feel about her, the way I think about her, it's different from how it was with Jamie. She's my friend, but there's something else, too. I imagine kissing her, and the image only makes my brain itch a little. I hold the picture in my mind, and then switch it to something easier. Holding her hand. I could do that. That would be nice, actually.

It's possible she meant the Gram the same way Jamie and I did when we sent them to each other. I'm her friend. But I think of that look in her eyes, the way her gaze drifted to my lips, and I know that's not why.

Again and again, I think about texting Jamie. He would know what to do. But he made his choice, and it wasn't me.

⸻

I'm in second period Monday, still ignoring Jamie, who keeps looking my way, when I get the text. I open it under the table.

Can we talk at lunch? Vanessa asks.

My heart jolts. Sure, I say back.

I find her in the art room, with a few other kids from QA. She leads me out, down the hall, toward the stairs, and we sit at the side of the top step. A few kids pass us on their way to the lunchroom, chattering and laughing.

"I have to tell you something," she says. I can hardly breathe. It feels like the world is rotating in front of me. "Did you get a CandyGram last week?"

"Yeah." I try to focus, to look her in the eyes. I'm not ready for this. "I know you sent it."

"Oh." She closes her mouth, glancing away down the stairs at a few QA kids coming up. She smiles at them and they wave and pass, and then she's looking at me again. "So. I guess I should tell you. I didn't send that to you as a friend. I sent it to you because I like you. I really like you."

I nod, clasping my knees with my hands.

"And I don't know. I thought maybe you liked me, too. It felt like we had this moment at our sleepover. I wanted to kiss you so bad. But then you got up and when you came back, everything was different." She chews on her bottom lip. "Do you like me back?"

I'm feeling five hundred emotions, all of them different, like I'm a planet caught between black hole and supernova. Either way, something is obliterated. Her eyes are fixed on my face, and I make my neck move so my head nods, because it feels like the only thing I can do, and then my words release like light into the stairwell.

"I do," I say. "I like you so much. I want to be near you all the time. I mean, not all the time, because that would be a lot, but I love being near you." Oh god. I said the L word. But she's smiling and it's out there and it's true. "You're an amazing friend and I want to be your girlfriend, too. I want to hold your hand and cuddle and talk every day."

Her hand grazes my cheek and curls around my neck and starts to pull me in and my body pulls back before I can think.

She drops her hand. "What's wrong?"

I shake my head. "I'm sorry. I just." I take a deep breath. "There's something I haven't told you."

She tilts her head, frowning, but it's an I-don't-get-it frown, not an angry frown. I will my heart to slow down.

"I think I might be . . ." I hesitate. "I might be asexual."

Her mouth forms a silent O and she sits back, just a little bit.

"I don't really know for sure. Sometimes I think kissing could be cool, but it also seems really weird to me, and I don't even like thinking about sex." I blush. "Not that I'm assuming we'd have sex. But I just think you should know before you date me. It won't be like a normal relationship."

She nods slowly. "Okay."

I watch her. "What are you thinking?"

"I think . . ." She looks at me. "I think you're amazing. And I don't think there's any such thing as normal. You exist, therefore you're normal."

I grin and reach for her hand, and she curls her fingers around mine.

And then she lets go. "But also. I like kissing. And I think about sex." She lets out a short laugh. "Like, a lot. So I think I need to take some time."

"Oh." Of course. I know what this means. "It's fine. You don't have to pretend for me."

"I'm not—"

"Come on." I let out a sharp laugh and she pulls back a little. "It wouldn't work anyway. Just go find someone you can have sex with."

"What?" She frowns, like maybe she's angry, but I can't tell and I don't want to stick around and find out. I scramble up and jog down the stairs. My heart is pounding, and I have to get out of here. She doesn't call after me. It's Jamie all over again, but this time it hurts in a whole new way. Jamie ripped out my heart, discarded it like a weed. With

Vanessa, I could feel a new heart blooming, like the flower on her bedroom wall. I run down the stairs, and the farther away I get, the more my heart withers, until there's nothing but a husk. Enough to remember what was there, but not what having it felt like.

CHAPTER TWENTY-THREE

TUESDAY: LIBRARY.

CHAPTER TWENTY-FOUR

WEDNESDAY: LIBRARY.

CHAPTER TWENTY-FIVE

THURSDAY: LIBRARY.

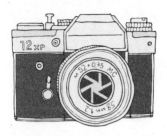

CHAPTER TWENTY-SIX

FRIDAY: LIBRARY.

The bus ride home: I wait in the girls' bathroom until the school is quiet. Until I know Vanessa is gone and on the first bus.

Home: Cold. Empty. Dad and Garrett both out. Dad with Will and their friends. Garrett with his.

My room: I lie in bed, curled in front of Netflix. Cartoons dance and fight and sing. I flip between tabs mindlessly, from the show to YouTube to my email and back.

I have a half-written email to Mom sitting on my screen every time I open that tab. I've been writing it in my head all week, then deciding not to, then writing it again, and now here it is, mostly typed out.

Looking at it makes me feel sick, and every time I go to type my name and hit send, I get a wave of anxiety so extreme I almost shut my laptop.

In the email, I apologize for not thanking her for the flowers, and then I say yeah, I'd love to come to San Francisco.

And it's not a total lie. I do want to visit San Francisco again. We took a family vacation there once and visited some of the galleries she'd helped open. I loved the city then, how magical it felt, the way everything smelled like the ocean.

I just don't want to live there. Not with her, anyway. But it feels like the only option. I mean, how do I turn her down? She'll be so angry. I can imagine how she'll react, how she might punish me for this betrayal, and it gets worse every time I picture it. Refusing to live with her would be way worse than just disagreeing with her.

And at this point, I don't see how I can stay here. Jamie picked Caroline. There's no way Vanessa will date me, especially not after the way I snapped at her. Every time I remember what I said, the look on her face, I feel this hot nausea in my stomach. And it's not like Marc and I are that close. Which leaves me with no one. If I leave, Dad will miss me, but he'll still have Garrett, and Garrett needs him. And I can come visit them anytime.

So maybe it will be better to go. Even if I have to live with Mom.

My phone pings. I glance at the screen and then I'm staring at it.

are you free right now

It's Jamie.

I open the phone and type so fast I hit send on a typo.

Wyh are you texting me?

Three dots. A text. i don't have anyone else

What are you talking about? Go kiss your girlfriend.

His face pops up on my screen and I let out a yelp before I realize it's just the photo I set for his number. He's calling me. I growl-scream. But I answer.

"I thought you said we couldn't hang out. Or did you get special dispensation?" I can hear how awful I sound, but I don't care.

"Arden." He's crying. All the bitterness in my mouth liquefies into fear. "Please come."

"What happened?"

"Just come. As fast as you can."

"Okay. Okay." I'm on my feet, shoving feet into sneakers, shrugging into my parka. I'm in my sweats, but it doesn't matter. "Where are you?"

"I'll text you the address. I have to go."

"Jamie!"

He's gone. A second later, my phone lights up with a

text. I'm out in the hallway, to the window, seeing Dad's car at the curb, running to his room and finding the keys, sprinting out the door, starting the car, peeling away. I don't even feel nervous. Jamie needs me. I'm going to North Seattle.

The house is a real Craftsman, not like Marc's rich-people imitation. It's on a quiet side street near the school. I step out of the car and the smell of pine trees fills the air.

The front room is dark, but through the window in the door I can see there's a light on in the hallway. I mount the front steps and stand there for a moment, and then I knock.

No answer.

I knock again, louder, harder. I don't know why, but I get the urge to shout Jamie's name, so I do.

A minute later, he opens the door and throws himself at me, hugging me tight. And behind him, Caroline appears in the hallway.

"Where are you going?" she says. Her voice is loud, her eyes wide. "I told you not to hang out with her."

"I'm leaving," Jamie says.

"You can't leave." She moves forward, flipping on the lights. "You can't leave me." She's crying now. "You're breaking my heart."

"This isn't right," Jamie says, his voice wavering. "Every time I try to break up with you, you tell me you can't live without me. That's not healthy, Caro."

"I need you." She's walking toward us. I step down, pulling on his arm. He steps down after me. She looks at me for the first time. "You fucking bitch. This is all your fault."

"Fuck you." I spit the words at her. "You're a liar. Let's go, Jamie." I tug on his arm and he follows me down the rest of the steps. She calls his name, and he flinches but keeps walking.

"Come on," I say, low and soft, folding my hand around his. Fuck what she thinks. Friends can hold hands, too. I love Jamie, and I'm not letting him go. "Almost there."

He swipes a hand across his eyes. I hit the button and the car unlocks and we get in and shut the doors, Caroline still calling his name, screaming it now.

In seconds, her voice fades, and we turn the corner. I'm breaking the speed limit, but I don't care. I want to get away from her, get Jamie away from her, as fast as possible.

Eventually, he speaks. "Thanks."

I can't find the words, so I just nod, white-knuckled on the steering wheel.

"Can we go to your house?" he asks.

I nod again.

We're almost there when he pulls out his phone. "Fuck. She's blowing me up."

I find my voice. "Turn it off."

"I can't just turn it off. What if she . . . what if she does something?"

"What?" I scan for another parking spot; the one in front of our house is taken. "Jamie. Are you serious?"

"When I tried to end it before, she cut herself." He stares at his phone as he says it. I find a spot at the end of the block and park.

His phone buzzes again. I reach out and take the phone, and he doesn't stop me. Caroline's picture flashes on the screen and I hit ignore. "Jamie. That's not your fault."

"If I hadn't, she wouldn't have." His voice is going jagged again, tears spilling over.

The phone buzzes again. I ignore the call again. "She didn't have to. She chose to do that. You didn't put the razor in her hand."

"I just don't understand." He's crying again, so hard I can barely understand him. "I did everything she wanted and it was never enough. I did everything."

"You shouldn't have to," I say. The phone buzzes. I turn it off. He's crying too hard to notice. "Jamie. Listen to me."

"I even fucked up our friendship," he sobs. "I fucked up our friendship because I was scared to lose her."

"Jamie." I grab his hand. "Look at me."

He does, through swollen eyes.

"I'm here. I'm not going anywhere."

"Okay," he whispers.

Inside the house, he curls up on my bed, and I sit behind him, resting my hand on his shoulder.

"It was so good at first," he says. "She's so funny and sweet. She was. She is. I don't know. It changed. Not all the time. But she would get so jealous and accuse me of cheating on her. Not just with you. With her friends. She was fixated on Emma for some reason. I think because she thought Emma was friends with you. She kept trying to make me give her my passwords. She said that was the only way I could prove to her I wasn't cheating."

"That's fucked-up." I squeeze his shoulder.

"I didn't. I tried to break up with her before. A couple times. When you saw me in the art hallway. I tried to end it the night before. She told me—" His voice cracks. "She told me she'd kill herself if I left her. She'd already showed me the cuts she made the last time."

"Jamie." I wrap my arms around him, one over his chest, the other under his neck, and he grips my arm tight. "I'm so sorry. It's not your fault."

"I know that logically. I remember the Power and Control Wheel. But I still feel like it is. I just wanted . . ." A sob shakes loose. "I can't believe I let that happen."

"It's not your fault," I tell him again, and again, as he cries. "You didn't deserve it. You didn't do anything wrong." I want to say it until it's imprinted in his brain, until he believes it, but he cries and cries until he's coughing.

When the tears pass, he's quiet for a while in my arms, and then he slowly sits up. I grab a roll of toilet paper from the bathroom and a wet washcloth and bring it to him.

"I just don't know what to do now," he says, pressing the cloth to his face. "I'm not going back to her. But I don't know what she's going to do next."

"Have you told your moms?"

He shakes his head.

"Jamie. You have to tell them."

He starts tearing up again. "It's so embarrassing."

"They won't think that. They love you."

"My mom—Lisa—her ex-husband, he was abusive. I got the relationship talk along with the sex talk. And I still messed up." He crumples the comforter in his hands.

"Jamie." I grab his shoulders, ducking my head down so I can look him in the eye. He avoids me. "You did not mess up. Caroline is the one who messed up. Please believe me."

"I'm so sorry I didn't before." He's crying again. "I don't know what I was thinking. I was such an asshole."

"It's not your fault. She was controlling you."

"Still. What I said about you being aro-ace. I know it's not like that. You're the best friend I've ever had. You understand love better than most people."

"I mean. I don't think I'm aromantic."

He looks up at me. "What?"

"I kind of . . . like someone." I squirm and look away. "I still don't want to have sex. But like. I want to cuddle her and hold her hand. And maybe kiss. Maybe."

"Oh my god. Who?"

So I tell him about Vanessa, and Photography Club, even about hanging out with Marc (but not the part where

Marc came out to me). Jamie listens with hands clasped together, gasping and cooing in all the right places. When Vanessa cuts my hair, he swoons back onto the bed.

"Your hair does look fucking cool," he says.

"I know, right?" I grin, fluffing my bangs. But the grin doesn't last long. I tell him about the CandyGram, and my talk with Vanessa.

"Wait." He holds up a finger. "You assumed that her taking time to think about it meant no?"

"Was I supposed to take it another way?"

"How about face value?"

I shrug, shifting on the bed, twisting my mouth.

"Just give her a chance," he says.

"I guess."

He asks to stay over that night, and I don't even have to think about it. He uses my phone to let his moms know, and I hear Kim pause when he says he's at my house. I can't make out her words, but she sounds surprised.

"I know," he says. "We're cool now." He smiles at me. "Yeah, I thought so, too, but I'm not. I'll tell you about it later. I want to talk to both of you."

"You thought what?" I ask when he hangs up.

"I was supposed to stay over at Caroline's." He jumps onto the bed beside me.

I raise an eyebrow. "Her parents were cool with that?"

He nods, and then his mouth curves into a mischievous smile. "I mean, it's not like I could get her pregnant."

"Good point."

A few hours later, there's a soft tap on my door, and Dad pushes it open. Jamie looks up from *Steven Universe* and waves.

There's an awkward pause for a second, and then Dad recovers. "Haven't seen you in a while," he says. Jamie shrugs. "You staying the night?" he asks. Jamie nods.

"How was hanging out with Will?" I ask.

Dad smiles. "It was great." We look at each other a moment longer, and he seems like he wants to say something, but he doesn't.

I break the silence with a giggle. "Okaaaay, good night, Dad." He smiles and shuts the door.

"How's everything with your mom?" Jamie asks.

Mom. The email. The showdown with Caroline wiped it from my brain. I pause the show.

"She contacted us."

Jamie sits up. "No way."

I pull up the email, closing out my draft, and show him Mom's message.

"Wow," he says, reading it. "What are you going to do?"

"I don't know." I tell him about the divorce papers, and the counseling. "I mean, it's been five months of nothing, and now this?"

"It's not even a real apology," he says. "'I'm sorry if that was hurtful to you'? Why doesn't she just apologize for her own actions instead of apologizing for how you might feel about them?"

"That's true." I stare at the screen, then push the laptop away, closing it. "I don't want to live with her, Jamie. But she's my mom. Am I supposed to not talk to her for the rest of my life?"

He watches me as I lie there, staring up at the ceiling, and then lies down beside me.

"I just wish I understood why she left. I feel like it was our fault somehow. Like we didn't meet her expectations. Like, no matter what, we were never good enough."

Jamie grabs my hand. I know he understands.

"It's not your fault," he says. "If I didn't do anything wrong, then neither did you."

I squeeze his hand. Even though I said the same to him, it's harder to believe when I'm saying it to myself. But it's better than the alternative. In the absence of proof I know will never come, trusting myself is the only choice I have.

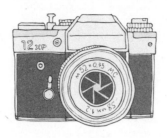

CHAPTER TWENTY-SEVEN

OVER THE NEXT WEEK, JAMIE AND I HANG OUT EVERY DAY. WE have a lot of time, because it's midwinter break and we don't have any school for a week. Which is a relief to both of us. I don't have to face Vanessa, and Jamie can avoid Caroline. He blocks her number Monday, and then has to block her on Instagram and Twitter, too, because she switches to messaging him there. His moms are supportive, just like I thought they'd be, and Lisa puts in an angry call to Caroline's mom. We don't know if it works. Jamie doesn't want to unblock her and find out.

But blocking Vanessa isn't an option for me, because I want to hear from her. I know I walked away from her out of fear, and I wish more than anything I could do that moment over. But reaching out feels wrong. She said she wanted time to think, and I respect that.

And if I'm being honest, I'm scared to reach out.

On Wednesday, I'm getting ready to meet up with Jamie, who said he wanted to go somewhere today but refused to tell me where, only that we'd be inside. The day is cloudy, but it doesn't look like rain, so I have my blazer on over my hoodie instead of my raincoat.

When I come into the kitchen to grab a snack before heading out, Garrett is there, eating cereal.

"Hey," I say, and he gives me a nod back, eyes fixed on his phone.

I riffle through the fridge and grab a yogurt, then a spoon, and it's so tempting to just go back to my room, but I'm tired of all the silence. So I slide into the stool across from Garrett.

He exhales a sigh, but I ignore it. "What's up?"

He shrugs.

I don't want to ask him about counseling, or whether he's still drinking, or whatever he and Dad talked about. I don't want to seem like Mom, always questioning and prodding, all over again.

But there is one thing I can ask him about.

"Have you checked your email?" I know he hardly ever does, except for school, and only when Dad reminds him.

He looks up at me warily. "Yeah."

"Did you see the one from Mom?" I try to say it as casually as possible, mixing the fruit chunks in the yogurt, not looking at him.

His voice is quieter this time. "Yeah."

"Did you email her back?" I ask. I look at him. His eyes are fixed on me, and I realize how long it's been since we really made eye contact. He looks hesitant, but hopeful.

He shakes his head. "Did you?"

"I haven't yet." After that day with Jamie, I deleted my draft. I don't know when I'm going to write another one. Part of it is petty: I want her to know how it feels to wait, to wonder, to hurt. If it hurts her at all.

But I also don't know what to say. I know that when it comes down to it, I don't want to live with her, and I can tell her that, but leaving it at just that feels weird. Like I should say more. Like I should tell her how I feel about the way she treated us. I have a right to. But that doesn't feel good, either.

"I'm not going to go live with her," he says. His shoulders are squared, drawn up a little, like he's waiting for backlash.

"Same," I say. "The way she treated us . . ." I take a deep breath. "It was messed-up."

Neither of us says anything for a long moment. Garrett rests his fingers on his phone, staring at the dark screen, but doesn't pick it up. Outside, the clouds shift for a just a minute and the kitchen lights up with sunlight, and just as quickly it fades again.

Then he nods, and his shoulders lower, just a little bit. "Cool jacket," he says.

I smile. "Thanks."

<hr>

Jamie and I meet on the corner. He's bouncing on the balls of his feet, swaying back and forth to the music in his big headphones, and grins when he sees me, taking the headphones off.

"You ready?"

"Not really," I say with a smirk. "Since I have no idea what you're plotting."

"Don't worry," he says. "You'll like it."

We walk down Broadway. At the south end of the street, just after the Pike/Pine corridor, he turns left abruptly, and suddenly I know where we're going. At least, I think I know. I haven't been back since that night, and my chest tightens. My hands are clammy, and I stick them in my pockets to warm them. Jamie strides along, smiling, and I try to keep pace as we reach a series of run-down buildings.

And then there we are, in front of a small glass door. The handmade sign is gone. There's one with neon cursive in its place: RIOT GALLERY.

"Oh my god," I say. "Jamie."

He puts a hand on the door and turns to me. "I brought you here because I need to apologize."

Tears spring to my eyes, but I keep looking at him.

"I shouldn't have missed your gallery opening." The sideways smile is gone and his face is serious now, his stare direct and gentle. "I'm really sorry, Arden."

"It's okay," I whisper, the words a habit, but I know it's not true as soon as I say them.

Jamie shakes his head. "No, it's not."

"You were being manipulated."

He shrugs. "Yeah. And I still wish I'd been there. I wish I'd stood up to her. If I had—" He stops, swallowing and blinking.

I take a deep breath. I know what I need to say. "I wish things had been different, too. It really . . . it really hurt me, Jamie." My voice cracks a little. "It felt like you picked her over me. I know that I didn't react the best, and I'm sorry, too. I missed you so much, and I didn't know what to do. I thought our friendship was over forever—" He steps toward me and we hug, tightly, like our arms are a circle of protection nothing can break.

"You're my best friend," he says in my ear. "I love you."

"I love you, too, Jamie," I choke out, and then I'm sobbing into his fleece jacket.

We hold each other for a long time, and eventually the tears stop. I take a deep breath, and I feel his chest and back swell like he is, too, and we step away from each other.

"Ready?" he asks, smiling again.

I nod, and he pushes the door open.

When we enter the gallery, Ryan looks up from the desk next to the door.

"Arden! So nice to see you." He tilts his head, studying Jamie. "And you . . . you look familiar." He puts a hand to his heart. "You're the subject!"

Jamie strikes a pose, grinning, and then we all laugh. I grab his arm and drag him across the gallery, through the hallways, until we round the corner and he stops.

"Oh my god." He stares at his photo, glowing under the light. "It's huge!"

That smile, the grin I've captured in so many photographs, breaks out across his face again. "Holy shit." He steps forward, up to the picture, leaving me standing and watching him there, looking up into his own face, into his own eyes fixed on the small bottle in his hand, the descent of the testosterone into the needle, the focus and wait in his stare at the moment before injection.

He turns and looks at me. "I told you."

"What?"

He grins again. "You're going to be famous."

I step up beside him, and he sidles over and links his arm through mine, resting his head on my shoulder. "I'm sorry, Arden. Next time I date someone, I won't get so sucked in."

"I mean . . . you might." I lean my cheek on his hair. "I get it. You were really excited about her."

"Still. I could do better."

"In multiple ways," I say, dryly, and he laughs.

"That's for sure."

"Next time, I'll tell you right away if something's bothering me," I say, and he squeezes my arm. We stand there for a while, gazing up at the picture, just looking.

I stare at my computer screen Sunday night, Dr. Benjamin's words echoing in my head, his kind face smiling at me from his chair. We had another appointment yesterday, and I told him about the email, how I didn't know what to say, didn't know how to confront her.

"Do you have to confront her now?" he asked. He's good at asking questions. Sometimes it's annoying; I just want him to give me the answer. I can tell he knows what to do.

I shrugged. "No?"

"You sound unsure."

"I feel like I'm supposed to."

"Why's that?"

I fiddled with the squishy ball he keeps in a dish of fidget toys on his bookcase. "Well, how she treated us was wrong. When people do something wrong, you have to stop them."

"Why is it your job to stop her?"

I shrugged again.

"What would you say if you didn't feel like you had to stop her?"

"I don't know. Probably just tell her that I'd rather stay in Seattle."

"That's a fine answer." He smiles at me. "Arden, we're approaching the end of our time today. Between now and next session, I want you to write two emails, in your Word program or Notes app or whatever is most comfortable, so you don't accidentally send it. In one, I want you to really lay into her. Just tell her everything you want to say, without worrying about the consequences. In the other one, just write the version you'd write if you decided it's not your job to hold her accountable."

"Okay." I shrug again. I know I must look like a typical sullen teenager, but I don't totally understand this assignment. He's given me homework before, but usually just an idea or a thought to ponder. "What do I do with them?"

"Nothing. They're just for you."

I already wrote my first email. The one where I tear into her. The assignment sounded corny, but it actually felt good to say it all, for once. And I don't have to worry about what she'll say back.

Weirdly, the second one is harder. It feels so stilted and awkward, to try and just answer the facts of the email.

Hi Mom. Thanks for the flowers. They were beautiful. Thank you for inviting me to live with you, but I am going to stay in Seattle. I hope you have a good day.

Love, Arden

The email feels like a lie, like I'm going along with her game. And I know she'll find a way to get mad at me anyway, probably for not accepting her invite. There's no way to win.

But she's my mom. Why is it my responsibility to make her feel okay, to help her change?

I stare at the second email, and then I copy it, paste it into the blank email reply box, and hit send before I can overthink. She can say whatever she wants. This is my decision.

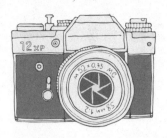

CHAPTER TWENTY-EIGHT

THE FIRST MONDAY BACK TO SCHOOL, I TEXT VANESSA.

Hey. Can we talk today?

Sending the text floods me with anxiety, but her response is immediate. Totally. With the pink flower emoji.

Weaving toward her locker at lunch, I see her before she sees me, and she's so beautiful, I can hardly look at her. Her hair is loose around her shoulders, no lipstick today, eyes glowing in the sunlight.

She smiles when she sees me walking toward her, but she looks hesitant. "Hi. How was your break?"

"It was . . ." I pause. "It was a lot."

"Oh yeah?" She tucks a loose strand of hair behind her ear, looking at me.

"Yeah. I, um, that's not why I want to talk, though."

"Do you want to find somewhere quiet?"

"That would be good."

It's sunny out, and weirdly warm, so we go outside, to a bench beside the front doors of the school. I want to say what I need to say before we unpack our lunches, in case it doesn't go well and she doesn't want to sit with me afterward.

We sit facing each other, and she waits.

"I owe you an apology," I say. "The way I talked to you that day wasn't cool."

She nods, her face serious now. "Yeah. If I wanted to just have sex with someone, I would do that."

"I know." I force myself to keep looking her in the eye. I'm not avoiding things anymore. "I'm really sorry."

"Why did you say that?"

I fiddle with the hem of the jacket. "I thought that you 'thinking about it' was just you trying to let me down easy."

"Definitely not," she says. She traces a finger over the lines of a small graffiti tag on the bench between us. "I really wish you hadn't run away like that, Arden."

"I know," I say. "I wish I hadn't either. And I understand if you don't want to date me. For any reason."

She takes a deep breath. "I've thought about it a lot. I know we're different, and want different things out of a relationship."

Here it comes.

"But we also fit, in so many ways." She smiles. "You make me laugh. You've got such amazing artistic vision, and you're such a good friend. You're kind and open. My parents like you."

The tears are blurring my eyes and I blink them away. I'm looking right into her eyes, but I'm not drowning. I'm flying.

"There are lots of ways to have a relationship without sex. And we can talk about that. I want to be with you. Arden Grey, will you be my girlfriend?"

I can't speak, just nod, the tears spilling over.

"Can I hold your hand?" she asks, and I reach out and grab hers, surprising a laugh from her beautiful mouth.

She laces her fingers through mine and moves closer, resting her head on my shoulder. "How does this feel?"

It's nice. Her hand is warm, and even though my heart is freaking out, it's not the bad kind of freaking out. I don't feel like running. I feel anchored. I smile and squeeze her fingers.

"I'm going to assume that means good things," she says.

"We're holding hands," I say, and she giggles.

"You have no idea how long I've wanted this," she says.

"Really?"

"Arden." She pulls back and looks at me. "Since the minute I saw your photo."

"I promise I won't run away like that again," I say.

She squeezes my hand. "Thank you."

"I want you to meet someone," I say. "My best friend. Jamie."

"I remember him. You two used to hang all the time. I thought you were dating."

"Everyone thought that." I roll my eyes. "No. We had a fight. We're okay now. It's a long story."

She nods.

"I was thinking he could hang with us at lunch."

She smiles. "Of course."

I'm sprawled in the easy chair that night, watching Garrett blow zombie heads off, when I notice Dad standing in the hall doorway. He leans on the doorframe, a half smile on his face.

"What's up?" I straighten. Garrett doesn't look up from his game.

"I need to talk to you kids about something." He comes in and sits on the coffee table.

Garrett's still going apeshit on the zombies. Dad reaches over and waves a hand in front of his face. With a sigh, Garrett pauses the game and sits back on the couch.

Dad looks at both of us, hands clasped in his lap, and takes a deep breath. "So, you know that I spent a lot of time in this neighborhood when I was in college. Before I met your mom."

Garrett and I nod, glancing at each other.

"And that I had a lot of gay friends."

Garrett's leg is bouncing up and down.

"I loved your mom." Dad's eyes shine a little bit, and he blinks. "But I'm not just attracted to women."

The music of the game on pause tinkles through the quiet living room. Garrett grabs the controller and I almost say something, but he saves the game and turns off the television.

"So . . ." He looks at Dad. "You like guys, too?"

"There's more than just guys and girls," I say.

He rolls his eyes. "I know that."

Dad cracks a smile. "I think gender doesn't really matter to me. But yes, I'm attracted to men as well."

"You're dating someone," Garrett says. "Is it that Will guy?"

"Maybe I should have let you do my coming-out speech!" Dad says. His eyebrows draw down and for a second I think he's angry, but then he bursts out laughing.

Garrett and I look at each other, and Garrett shrugs. "It was kind of obvious."

"Not to me," I say. It didn't occur to me that Dad would start dating again. But of course, that's part of breaking up. Eventually people find someone new, if that's what they want. And now that I think about it, I remember all those random times he seemed so happy, even when stuff with Mom was bad. He was probably happy because of Will.

Dad quiets, wiping his eyes. "How do you feel about it?"

"It's okay." I shrug. I pick at the arm of the chair, trying to imagine Dad with this faceless Will, who in my head looks like an off-brand Adam Rippon. Try to picture them kissing. It's weird, but not because it's my dad kissing a guy. My dad kissing anyone is weird, because kissing is weird in general, and especially when it's your parents doing it. "It's fine." I smile. "Actually, yeah. Um. It's fine with me because I'm dating someone, too. My friend Vanessa."

Dad grins. "I wondered."

"Well, I'm straight," Garrett says.

"Thank you for telling us," Dad says solemnly. "I accept you as you are, my son."

Garrett rolls his eyes but smiles anyway.

"So, we're good?" Dad looks at both of us.

I nod, and so does Garrett.

"Will wants to meet you both," Dad says. "I'm thinking a family dinner sometime soon."

"Cool. Can I play my game now?" Garrett asks.

Dad eyes him. "Only if I can play, too."

Garrett tosses him a controller, and motions at me with the third one. I hesitate. He raises his eyebrows, waving it at me again, and I take it from him. The three of us sit side by side on the couch, Dad in the middle, waiting for the game to start.

Now that she and Jamie are broken up, Caroline ignores me in Mr. Bones's class. But I'm fine with that. She's leaving Jamie alone for now.

Near the end of the week, I figure out why. I'm just coming up to my locker before lunch when the loudest laugh ever startles me and I look down the junior hall to see her, head tilted back, hand on Tanner's arm.

He's got that stupid smug grin on, and she flips her ponytail. They're talking to each other, but I'm too far away to hear the details, and then a surge of students fills the hallway and blocks my view.

I open my locker and grab my lunch. It's fine if she's moved on already, it's none of my business, and whatever gets her to back off of Jamie, honestly—but I almost feel sorry for Tanner.

Actually, if I'm being real, I feel sorry for both of them. They don't have to act like they do. They can make different choices.

But it's not my responsibility to help them.

I close my locker and head away down the hall.

"Arden!" I turn and see Emma fighting through the crush of kids toward me. "How are you?"

"Hey," I say, a little wary. "I'm okay. How are you?"

"Ugh." She rolls her eyes. "I've been better."

"What happened?" Emma was the one good thing about those lunches spent with Caroline's friends, and it's nice to talk to her again, even if I'm not sure why she's talking to me.

"Our friend group kind of blew up." She makes a poof motion with her hand. "I tried to talk to Caroline about how she was treating Jamie, and she didn't want to hear it, and everyone took sides . . . It was messy."

"Oh wow."

"Yeah. Anyway, I was thinking about you, and hoping you were okay, and I kind of wondered . . ." She pauses, and for the first time since I've known her, she looks a little shy. "Do you want to hang out at lunch?"

"I'm actually going to the art room," I say. "But . . . do you want to come with? I hang out there with the Queer Alliance kids, and Jamie and some other people."

She grins. "I would love that."

On Sunday morning, I wake up before my alarm. Normally, I wouldn't set one on the weekend, but today is special. Today, I'm going hiking.

It was Marc's idea. Apparently, it's something his family likes to do whenever his parents are in town. He texted me Friday night, all stoked about it, and I texted Jamie, and then Vanessa, because why not? All the people I'd most want to spend time with, all together. Maybe Emma will become one of those people, too.

We went camping almost every summer when I was a kid. Mom and Dad used to go all the time before we were born, or so they told us every time we headed out, the car packed to the ceiling with gear and food. They were happy then, or at least it seemed like they were—or maybe I just didn't notice either way because I was too busy splashing in whatever lake or river we camped beside and bossing Garrett around. I don't know if it matters, anyway. Those memories are happy ones, and I want to hold on to them.

I roll out of bed and get dressed, throwing a raincoat, a hat, and gloves into my backpack, along with my camera. It's not raining outside, but the weather might be different in the mountains. In the kitchen, I grab an apple and the sandwich I made the night before, pour a bowl of cereal, and carry it all back to my room, almost spilling the milk on my carpet before setting everything on my desk. The snacks go in my backpack, and I sit in my desk chair, gobbling down the cereal. They'll be here any minute.

On the wall above me, the softball player stretches back, frozen forever. I stare up at the picture, the cereal exploding cinnamon in my mouth. I don't like this photograph. I've never liked it. It's not a terrible photo. The woman in it does look powerful, just like Mom said. But she's not the kind of powerful I want to be, and whatever Mom felt when she looked at it, I don't feel that.

I finish the cereal. Standing up, I pluck the tacks out of the corners of the poster and pull it off the wall, rolling it up and pushing it under the bed. The spot on the wall is bare, but that's okay. I'll find something else to fill it.

My phone buzzes. I grab my pack and hustle out the door.

"Arden!" Jamie's shriek echoes down the block, his whole upper body out the window of Marc's car as it skids to a stop at the curb. I jump off the stoop, grinning, and stride toward the car. Marc leans back and fist-bumps me as I slide into the backseat. I look at Vanessa, already there, and she smiles, grabbing my hand.

"Hi." Her brown eyes sparkle. Marc grins at us in the rearview mirror.

"That's what I like to see," he says. "Love is in the air."

I blush, and Vanessa giggles. But the word doesn't feel wrong, or confusing. Maybe this is love. Maybe I'll find out.

The drive is long, taking us out of Seattle along I-90. The city fades quickly, the ridges rising around us, green with pine trees, cloaked in low-hanging clouds. When we arrive at the trailhead, the parking lot is almost full. We slide into the last open space. Jamie breaks out the snacks: Kim's homemade energy bars.

Going up, we pass one group after another coming down, people who got an early start. Young, fit-looking professional types, older couples, a few families with young children. We're loud, talking and laughing, and we get a few glares, but smiles, too. Indulgent smiles, as if we're the cutest thing ever. Eventually, the trail quiets, and it's just us, climbing upward. The clouds start to thin, watery sunlight peeking through the breaks. It's colder up here, but we're warming up.

Marc forges ahead, his long legs taking him faster than us. Jamie strolls behind him, and Vanessa and I follow, holding hands as we step around roots, only letting go when the trail gets too narrow for two. We emerge from the tree line onto a bare, rocky section of ridge, the highway and the river far below.

"We're getting closer!" Marc calls back, and we cheer raggedly.

The trees appear again as we round a switchback. Marc and Jamie disappear under dark green branches. As Vanessa and I reach the forest, I almost trip. My shoelace is untied, trailing behind my boot. I kneel down, camera bumping my leg as I lace up.

"Arden!" Vanessa's whisper behind me makes me look up and I see it: a deer, stepping delicately through the trees, down toward the path. I freeze. It hasn't seen us yet. A breeze plays cool and soft around my ears.

Carefully, I lift the camera to my eye, keeping my

movements slow and smooth. I look through the viewfinder and see the deer, on the path now. It goes utterly still, and so do I. Don't run, please. Just one second more. As the deer turns and looks directly at me, I trip the shutter and take the photo—just before the deer leaps away into the brush.

I lower the camera and stare after the deer until the sound of it crashing away is gone. I realize I'm grinning, my heart swelling like a balloon, like it can carry me away over the valley. Vanessa comes up beside me.

"That was . . ." Her voice trails off. "That's your National Geographic moment right there."

"Yeah," I say, still grinning. I can't wait to develop it. I can't wait to submit it. She slips her hand into mine and we walk onward together, into the trees.

Dear Reader,

There are multiple abusive relationships in this book. The way Arden's mother treats each member of her family is abusive, and the way Caroline treats Jamie is abusive. While the flavor of behavior and tactics vary relationship to relationship, they all qualify as abuse.

Arden, Garrett, their dad, and Jamie each deal with and eventually begin to extricate themselves from their abusive relationship, and that makes them survivors. I am a survivor, too, of multiple abusive romantic relationships.

Anyone can be abusive, regardless of gender or sexuality, and can enact abuse in any kind of relationship, whether it's romantic, platonic, or familial. It takes many forms, and these forms are often outlined in what's called the Power and Control Wheel. This is a tool developed by survivors to showcase the different tactics people who abuse others use to control their victims. Garrett, Jamie, and Arden are all familiar with this wheel thanks to their school health classes, and this helps them identify what's happening in their relationships.

Whether you have concerns about a relationship in your life or not, this wheel can help you learn to identify warning signs. The URL on the following page will take you to the wheel on the website of New Beginnings, a

Seattle-based domestic violence organization. This wheel is interactive, and you can click through different parts to learn about different forms of abuse. There are additional resources below the URL if you or someone you know want to talk to a professional, and for thinking about what constitutes healthy relationships.

Thank you for reading this book. You deserve to feel safe, loved, and respected in all your relationships.

—R.S.

THE POWER AND CONTROL WHEEL

www.newbegin.org/learn-more/what-is-domestic-violence/

IF YOU OR SOMEONE YOU KNOW NEEDS HELP

Contact the National Domestic Violence Hotline
Call 1 (800) 799–7233
Text START to 1 (800) 799–7233
Live Chat: www.thehotline.org/

WHAT IS A HEALTHY RELATIONSHIP?

www.thehotline.org/resources/healthy-relationships/

Acknowledgments

Thank you to everyone who supported me and this book on our way to publication.

My wonderful agent, Lauren Abramo, and my talented editor, Maggie Lehrman: You see the heart and soul of my characters and their stories. The team at Abrams: my cover designers, Hana Anouk Nakamura, Chelsea Hunter, and Deena Fleming; managing editor, Marie Oishi; proofreader, Margo Winton Parodi; copy editor, Ashley Albert; the publicity and marketing dynamos Brooke Shearouse, Jenny Choy, and Patricia McNamara O'Neill; Jenn Jimenez in production; Emily Daluga, for the editorial assistance; and of course my publisher, Andrew Smith. Being an Abrams author is a dream because of all of you. Thank you for the talent and hard work each of you brings to this book.

I'm so grateful to Tin House for your hand in supporting this book and my career so far. Lance, India, Molly, and the readers for the 2019 Tin House YA Fiction Workshop, thank you for bringing me into such a wonderful and vital literary community. To the super-talented 2019 THYA cohort and our fearless faculty, Lilliam Rivera, Morgan Parker, and Nina LaCour: learning with you and from you was a gift that keeps on giving. And especially Team Mommy Issues: Joni, Angie, Lauren, Kristen, and Cassie. I'm so happy we met and have kept up the literary fellowship. Thank you to Nina LaCour for your gentle and encouraging facilitation, and also for writing *We Are Okay*. Your delicate and resonant handling of complex familial themes inspired me to write this book.

Hayden, for being such a thoughtful and supportive sounding board for this book when it was still in the half-written development stages, and for your love and support of me and my career as it got off the ground.

Vanessa, for encouraging me to apply to Tin House, and for that joking conversation about me naming a character after you. I took it seriously, and turns out it was the perfect fit.

Natalie, for reading an early draft and giving me your valuable feedback as a YA reader.

All my friends and family, always, for all you do and who you are.

Emmett, for cheering me on and loving me so well through my debut year, the pandemic, and so much else. Building a partnership with you has been one of the biggest joys of my life. I love you more than words can say.

For my younger self. We survived, and we're thriving. I'm so proud of us.